The ARROW of TIME

PART ONE of
The Everyday Timekeeper's Almanac

B.T. Lamprey

CATCHALL
OTHER BIN
B O O K S

Catchall Other Bin Books, Berkeley

CATCHALL OTHER BIN BOOKS

The Arrow Of Time
Part one of *The Everyday Timekeeper's Almanac*
Copyright © 2022 B.T. Lamprey

Cover art and logo design by Jordan Collver

ISBN: 979-8-9873156-0-6 (paperback) / 979-8-218-07776-1 (ebook)

First published: 2022

10 9 8 7 6 5 4 3 2 1

Note: If you purchased this book without a cover, you may want to reconsider your purchasing habits. The cover does a great job protecting the pages, features beautiful art, and even includes a few jokes. Next time you buy a book, consider bringing a friend to help identify which books do and do not have a cover.

For Lee,
Far more wondrous than the first sprout of spring,
Generous as any autumn harvest,
And sharper than a winter's fiercest gale.
In every season, I remain yours.

CONTENTS

CALL OF THE KLAXON

A CENTURY or so after the apes first split the atom, much of Earth had been covered with coffee shops. Near the western coast of a particularly hard-hit continent, an over-caffeinated ape named Aloysius Cook died a hero. At least that's how history recorded the affair, and no one who knew the truth of the matter stuck around to correct the obituary.

For Aloysius, the day he died began as a perfectly ordinary Wednesday. The only thing remarkable on his schedule was a meeting about expense reports. As a search engine optimization specialist, and not a particularly seasoned one at that, Aloysius had never been in a position to file any expense reports. But when asked to attend a three-hour brainstorming session on the misuse of company resources, Al sighed, took a long sip from the discarded toner cartridge he used as a mug, and prepared himself for a wasted morning. At least there might be pastries.

Considering these meager expectations, Al was pleasantly surprised to find not only coffee and pastries in the twelfth-floor conference room, but an empty chair next to Lily from Legal. Al grabbed a spiral-bound packet and shuffled to his seat. Even as Martha from HR began to explain why a per diem system was preferable to line-item expense reports, Al felt a shiver of excitement run through him; Lily's electrifying presence was a stroke of luck that surpassed even the pastries.

After Al crammed his lanky frame into a chair and a Danish into his mouth, it took him a while to notice the paperback hidden inside Lily's spiral-bound packet. He could almost make out the title when she turned the page— something about Orleans. From the look of the sword-wielding woman on the cover, it was historical fiction. Al rifled through the cobwebbed filing cabinets of his memory to find the entry on "Orleans, Old." Hopefully he'd discover some tidbit he could use to start a conversation.

Al was so busy wracking his brain that he scarcely heard a word about the expense reports. He hardly noticed the air of boredom in the room, let alone caught the miasma of dread rolling through the halls like the smell of microwaved tuna from the breakroom. He was so preoccupied, in fact, that he entirely missed the faint screams.

Unseen as yet, catastrophe crept closer. Before the end of the hour, Aloysius Cook would be shot in the head. Who shoulders the blame for this tragedy remains a matter of considerable debate, but most historians agree it had something to do with all the guns. Really, the sheer number of guns just lying around was mind-boggling. To give you a sense of it, there were more than ten thousand guns around for every coffee shop.

Given this overabundance of firearms, it should come as no surprise that the killer got a gun without any fuss, by way of a loophole wide enough to accommodate a cruise ship. There's no compelling reason to chronicle his banal methods, or his feeble excuses; it's better to wipe the smear off the book and turn the page. Fittingly, the nonentity in question soon got the process started with his own ignoble death—thanks to a bit of help from Aloysius Cook.

Not that Al had any intention of killing someone, or even any thoughts vaguely in that direction. He was quite content contemplating Lily: her clever fingers, her sarcastic asides, her sly grin as she lingered over a particularly amusing passage in her paperback.

"Aloysius?" someone said. "Mr. Cook?"

Al looked up with a start and swiveled to the frustrated middle manager sitting at the far end of the table. A scowl scrunched Martha's face unpleasantly. Above her knitted brows a tight bun quivered. She was staring right at Al, and unless there was another Aloysius Cook sitting nearby, she seemed to have asked him a question. The uncomfortable silence stretched, and Martha's expectant gaze lingered. Al relinquished the last scrap of hope that her question was directed at the other, hypothetical Aloysius Cook.

"Is that a reasonable deadline?" Martha asked, apparently again.

Al took a second to gather his thoughts, and then a third.

Though Martha's attention was fixed firmly on Al, Phillip from Sales cleared his throat and squirmed like a schoolboy in need of the potty. *Shut up, Phillip,* thought everyone at once. The chorus of ill will radiating toward Phillip was so uniform that even the most ardent skeptic would have suspected telepathy was at work, if they hadn't already known just what a total tool Phillip was.

"My uncle used to say," Al began feebly, "that time and tide wait for no sailor."

Someone snorted.

"Was he a pirate?" Lily managed to ask before the giggling consumed her entirely. Her laughter sent a delightful tingle of anticipation running up Al's spine. He chuckled, losing himself in the little creases at the corners of her eyes.

Finally, Al dared turn back. Martha opened her mouth to speak, but paused before a sound had passed her lips. It was unsettling. The longer she waited to speak, the more unnerved Al became. Her silence had stretched well past awkward deliberation and right to the border of foreboding promise, when an astonishing racket intruded into the stillness—the blare of a klaxon.

This was startling for at least two reasons.

First, no one knew what a klaxon was exactly, except that it might have something to do with submarines. Seeing as they were on the twelfth floor of an office tower in downtown Oakland, the submarine theory was right out. But like pornography, a klaxon is unmistakable when it assaults the senses; the incessant blare was undoubtedly a klaxon.

Second, the klaxon was excruciatingly loud. It screamed over the soundscape like an incoming missile.

Before Al's eardrums could send in their two-weeks' notice, the klaxon stopped, and there was a strange hush, followed by the PA system's crackling declaration: "*This is an active shooter situation. Shelter in place. Lock all doors and windows. Wait for further instructions.*"

Everyone in the room turned to Martha from HR. Martha, finding she couldn't very well turn to herself, instead turned to the vague memories of the emergency preparedness seminar she'd attended the winter before last. What came to her most distinctly was an overwhelming sense of regret that she hadn't paid the least bit of attention to the seminar in question.

Martha settled on a show of confidence, and yelled, "Into the closet, and shut up!" Throwing aside spiral-bound packets and pastries, the gaggle of personnel stumbled toward the closet, toppling chairs in their haste. Across the room, Martha fumbled with the latch of the wide door leading to the hall and finally locked it. Then she strode to the overflowing closet, now in the process of disgorging obsolete electronics and packing in quite a lot of nervous employees. Martha shoved her prodigious bulk into that increasingly pungent shelter, heedless of propriety and dignity.

Aloysius Cook, still seated numbly in his small and uncomfortable chair, watched the bustle of his scrambling coworkers with astonishment. *Hang on,* he thought. *Should I be headed for the closet myself?*

"Al!" Lily shouted from what passed for shelter, a terrible urgency in her voice. "Can you grab my cell phone?"

Aloysius contemplated the squirming mass of humanity so awkwardly squished together in the storage closet. Before he could act—which might have taken a few more moments of deliberation—something even more surprising than a klaxon demanded his attention.

It sounded an awful lot like a gunshot.

Martha looked at the door to the hall. Now closed and locked, it offered no hint of whatever horror may or may not have been occurring in the hallway. To be on the safe side, Martha slammed the closet door shut. Aloysius found himself on the far side of that door, just as he'd nearly resolved to move toward it. He stood, considering his options.

The doorknob rattled. A moment later something slammed against the door.

Startled by the noise, a pack of undomesticated notions stampeded down the wide and untended boulevard of Aloysius' mind. Not all of the wayward thoughts concerned Lily, but a great many did. There were also quite a few about the casserole he'd had for dinner, which he hadn't much enjoyed the first time around. And suddenly he had a great new pitch for that startup conference he'd been mulling over. Eventually, a relevant thought stepped forward from the mob: *Get in the closet, idiot.*

Aloysius jumped over a fallen chair and careened toward the closet, hoping only to reach the relative safety of the herd.

The door to the hall flew open with a bang. As Aloysius turned back toward the noise, he slipped on someone's discarded spiral-bound packet and fell among the scattered chairs. From the floor, all he could make out were two leather boots stepping into the room. Aloysius began to crawl under the table but found the laces of his sneakers had caught on the spinning wheels of an overturned chair.

"I see you there." The unfamiliar voice dripped with menace. The boots paced closer.

An earsplitting blast shook the room, and the seat of an office chair exploded in a shower of foam and plastic. Al couldn't help but imagine his soft, moist, and irreplaceable body meeting the same fate.

Letting out a quiet moan, he struggled to disentangle his shoelaces. But no matter how frantically he shook his foot, he couldn't escape the clutches of the chair. His whole wonderful future would be wiped away because of a chair, and there was so much he'd been looking forward to. He'd even been planning to upgrade his phone that weekend. Two years locked in a contract, and now he'd never see a new phone again. "You goddamn bastard!" he cried at the chair. He rolled out from under the table, stumbled to his feet dragging the chair behind him, and with a final great wrench freed his foot from the shoe. "Not today!" he shouted in triumph.

Overbalanced, teetering, and wearing a single sneaker, Al stumbled backwards. He tripped over the assortment of pastries and tumbled across the table head over heels. Finding his feet miraculously beneath him at the end of a full flip, he thrust himself up like a swimmer pushing off the wall, slamming headfirst into the owner of the boots with a thud. Both of them fell amidst the spiral-bound packets. The pain in Al's skull was so intense and startling that he worried he might black out. Still, the gun was just sitting on the carpet between them.

Al reached for the instrument of death with one hand, pushing his assailant away with the other.

The gun thundered twice, and Aloysius stopped worrying.

2

PAPER CUTAWAY

KARL SKIMMED the news reports and obituaries on his screen with little interest and even less sympathy. It was one thing to watch helplessly as a Smilodon began to eat your still-living brother, or to feel the death throes of your beloved as the birth of a child ripped the last breath from her body. But this? There were trillions of strangers dead and tragedies soon forgotten. Karl was sure he could care less. Or was it, he *couldn't* care less? No matter. He didn't care about that, either.

Karl's thoughts bubbled uneasily, stewing in a sour broth of apathy and resentment. Reluctantly stirring his interest was an account in something called *The Nor Cal Gazette*. In it Karl had found a candidate for recruitment. But the find was only useful, and not just tedious, if it meant the end of his work for the day.

" . . . *Singlehandedly defending his company from a*

gunman . . . Shooter and hero both killed . . . Grateful coworkers recounted his final words of defiance and bravery." Karl grunted happily. No witnesses to the death, either, and only a few years before The Institute's planned incursion into the twenty-first century.

The decision seemed fairly cut and dried to Karl, but it wasn't his choice to make. Scratching his prodigious brow, he input the details into a standardized Extraction Request, a document almost as impersonal as Karl himself had become. Then, with a click, he was done.

His own duties discharged, Karl scratched himself in all the tender spots that troubled him. He gave far more attention to the itch on his upper back than he ever had to the death of a stranger.

Ah, right between the shoulder blades. It was turning out to be a rather satisfying morning.

KARL's brief deliberation was the sum total of the time and energy spent on the decision to pluck Aloysius Cook from the jaws of death. Karl's supervisor, Susan, didn't even bother to open the file. She knew that Karl had a sense for these things, and frankly she just wanted to be done with it. If she was going to pick a candidate today, Susan thought she might as well do it before lunch. That way she could enjoy her soup and salad without uncertainty roiling in her gut.

So the responsibility for that fateful decision traveled through the bureaucracy like a one-legged penguin riding an escalator—swiftly and directly from Karl up to Susan, then tumbling down haplessly to whoever had to clean up the mess today. Making that decision, pushing the proverbial penguin, was all Susan had to do. And Susan wasn't one to do much more than necessary.

Satisfied with her efforts, Susan felt like it might be a soup and sandwich day, after all. She could take her time munching, watch the dinosaurs for a bit. Maybe she'd get lucky, and a carnivore would eat something near the window.

———

WHEN THE FILE arrived in Joan's inbox, she pulled out the ancient copier and printed the damn thing. Warm paper in her hands, she flipped through the file with growing dismay, although she did at least like the paper. Paper was clean and predictable. Every sheet had the same width, the same height, the same thickness.

There was something else about paper—a terrible thing that Joan rarely admitted was a source of her fascination. *Paper would burn.* Hot and quick, like a courser given free rein in an open field. It felt good to watch the flame flicker. To feel the consuming heat, to smell the acrid smoke, to . . .

Joan knew better than to ruminate over bygones. She had been given a mission, and her considerable mental prowess would be focused on that alone. She'd have fifteen seconds to complete the extraction. It was more than enough, far more than enough. It had taken a four-person team for her own extraction, but that had been because the circumstances were extreme: the witnesses many, her death painful and slow, the exact timing of the end difficult to pin down.

They'd been late—too late. Too much was singed. On occasion she wondered whether they should have let her burn. Whether she'd have been better off without . . .

A decade had passed, and still she didn't like to think about it. *It.* It had already taken the future and the past. No need to let it have today. No need to remember the smell of the dry wood catching fire, the lick of the flames on her feet, the cries of a crowd hungry for her pain and humiliation.

Even The Institute at the Beginning of Time couldn't unmake her: There's only one shot at an extraction, even a botched one. Every timekeeper knew that just two overlapping incongruities could create a cascading causality breach with the potential to go critical. Sending multiple teams to the same space-time nexus was an unacceptable risk.

Why had they burned her in the first place? Had they really expected her to ride to battle in petticoats? No. They had expected her to scream piteously in her cottage while the foreign horde raped and pillaged their way across the countryside. And for refusing to cower, they had decided to kill her. It was hideously unfair.

It was also a monumental waste of Joan's talent and ambition, the kind of folly that only zealots could sanction. Ever pragmatic, The Institute had whisked her away and given her a home in the Cretaceous. Quite quickly she'd learned to operate in an entirely different environment.

Joan had already been a highly trained operative. She was a quick study. But the things she'd studied—Church Latin, medieval mixed-unit tactics, practical theology and the like—weren't of much use to her anymore. Still, she clung to the status quo with fervor. She needed to excel but found herself just scraping by. She wondered constantly what she was doing wrong. Convinced she'd fumbled more often than a drunk cardinal in a nunnery, she fretted over which misstep would be her last. Someone must eventually notice her bumbling.

But no one had. Joan began to catalogue every one of her errors, right down to spelling mistakes. Nobody else seemed to notice. No one said anything when she tripped or stuttered. In fact, no one berated her at all the first few days. A few weeks later, none had even mentioned her blunders. Eventually months passed without remark, and finally years had slipped by and all was quiet still. Joan's vast and exceedingly well-documented history of error had faced no oversight or scrutiny. Not one audit had presented itself. Not a single inspection had surprised her.

Joan resolved to do something about this lax attitude—later. It was a resolution Joan made frequently, faced as she was with a surfeit of incompetence. Joan believed that some unfortunate truths could not be denied.

The unfortunate truth plainly in front of her now was duty. She had no choice but to uphold it. So she approached this extraction with the same merciless attention to detail that had made her both an extraordinarily effective military leader and an incredibly annoying dance partner—not that she'd ever done much dancing.

On the other hand, she had spent quite a bit of time on the battlefield.

3

DISORIENTATION

THE FIRST THING Aloysius would remember after his escape from certain death was filling out some forms. It was extremely disconcerting, and also exactly what he should have expected.

"I need to ask you a few simple questions as part of the onboarding process," said a woman looking out the window. Al found himself roughly slouched on something cold and hard, blinking under harsh lights with all the assurance of an intern asking for a parking spot.

The woman by the window was sitting across from him at a small metal table. She had a name tag that read, "Hello! My name is JOAN," and an expression that said, "You're the reason I'm late for lunch." She shifted her gaze from the window to Al, then tried and spectacularly failed at reproducing a convincing smile. She turned back to the window.

Al blinked until his vision was clear and took a close look out the window himself. For a brief moment, he enjoyed the view of a nearby hill, verdant and picturesque. Then, everything came into focus.

On that hillside, Al happened to note, a tyrannosaur was devouring a triceratops with apparent satisfaction and no small amount of gore. Despite the fact that Aloysius had spent much of his childhood fantasizing about this very sight, he now found the reality of it frightening and more than a little messy. It was much as he'd felt after prom night.

"Are you seeing this?" Aloysius asked.

The young woman by the window turned to him with a moue, her short bob bouncing distractingly. Not distract-ingly enough to tear Aloysius' eyes from the tyrannosaurus pulling the steaming entrails from an eviscerated tricer-atops, but in other circumstances the sight would have been absolutely riveting.

In the distance, gore dripped from the tyrannosaur's jaws.

Joan pressed a button on the metal wall. The window grew opaque at once.

"You saw that, right?" Al asked, short of breath. "Are we safe in here?"

"We're safe," she said.

"What happened to me?" he squeaked, his breathing still ragged.

"Gunshot to the head."

"You mean . . . is this . . .?" Al looked around the room with a sinking sense of disappointment. At least it was air-conditioned, he noted with relief. Aloysius was fairly certain Hell wouldn't be air-conditioned.

He'd never been to Las Vegas.

"It's not the afterlife," Joan said. "I assure you."

"What was—"

"There will be time for questions," Joan said, shaking her head. "But first we have a standard procedure we need to get through as part of the onboarding."

"What am I boarding?" Aloysius checked for a ticket booth or a turnstile. Even a gangplank would have been a welcome sight.

"*Onboarding*," Joan said. With apparent distaste, she began to tap the screen of a small tablet.

"What?"

"You'll have an opportunity for questions after we finish these forms," she told him, her frown completely at odds with the pleasant tone of her voice.

"Why am I here?" Aloysius still hadn't heard much in the way of a response, but he thought he'd better keep trying. He prided himself on his persistence, and indeed his first and only pole-vaulting coach had once described him as "a caged bird that can't stop battering itself against the bars."

"Why are any of us here, for that matter?" Joan asked,

blowing a strand of hair away from her eyes. "I'd absolutely love to answer all of these fascinating questions, but we really need to get through this checklist so we can say we've dotted our i's and crossed our t's." She caught his eye and continued, "You know how it is."

By this time, Aloysius had taken his bearings without really meaning to. The room was small and sterile. He was sitting across from Joan. She was a short, handsome woman with short, dark hair. Her limbs were wiry, her hands callused, and she had that rare sort of self-possession that was often mistaken for grace. The lights flickered periodically, illuminating a stack of paper and a small, neatly folded pile of unremarkable cloth on an otherwise unadorned table.

"Let's get started," she said, all business. "Do you have any cybernetic implants or biomechanical devices on your person?"

"What?" Al asked. He was back to "What?" He felt mildly embarrassed about his lingering confusion. He would soon look back on the feeling with fondness and longing.

"Cybernetic implants or biomechanical devices. On your person," she repeated, enunciating slowly and clearly, as if the problem was that Aloysius was hard of hearing.

"I don't think so, no." He reached down to pat his pockets, but he didn't seem to have any. That was troubling. Where had he left them?

Joan gave him no time to consider the matter. "Have you formally studied history, philology, or physical anthropology or earned a degree in any related subject?"

"I was an English major," Al answered.

She raised her eyebrows. "That's not applicable," she said, shaking her head.

"Applicable to what?" Al asked in exasperation.

"Anything, really." Joan shrugged. "We'll count that as a no." She tapped on her tablet again. "Have you participated in any trivia contests?"

"Trivia?" Al parroted. "What do you mean?"

Joan nodded. "Also no." She input something on her tablet.

"It hardly seems important," Al continued.

"Just a few more. Have you worked in a professional capacity on or assisted in the creation of any encyclopedias, sports almanacs, or television viewing schedules?"

Al couldn't see what she was getting at. "Television viewing schedules?" he asked.

Joan sighed. "Encyclopedias, sports almanacs, or television viewing schedules?"

Al nodded as if understanding had come to him. "No. No to all three." He was beginning to get the hang of this.

"Good, good." Another few taps on the tablet. Then, "Come on," she said impatiently to the screen and looked up at him. "Sorry. You know how these things can . . ." She let the thought scurry away without pursuing it. "Okay."

She cleared her throat. "Have you ever interacted with a temporally displaced object or person?"

"I don't think so," he said. But her words had kindled an uneasy sensation in the back of his neck. How in the world would anyone know? And why was she asking? He began to look around the room for a hidden camera or a two-way mirror.

"Excellent." Joan tapped on her screen twice more. "We're in the home stretch now."

Hearing that, Al felt a bit more himself. Finally. He took a deep breath. "That's—"

"Are you sexually attracted to your own grandmother?" Joan asked, careful not to meet his eyes.

It took a moment for the question to register. "What?" Al said with revulsion.

"Are you sexually attracted to your grandmother?" she repeated, quite a bit louder and carefully emphasizing the consonants.

"Gramgram?" He felt increasingly sure there must be a camera somewhere close by, but damned if he could spot the thing. His gaze swiveled around the room.

"Yes." Joan looked down at her notes. "Do you find your 'Gramgram' to be sexually attractive?"

"Why would . . ." Al checked under the table. "Who are you to . . ." Nothing there either. "No! I'm not attracted to my grandmother."

"I don't just mean as an old woman," Joan added.

"When your 'Gramgram' was younger, was she attractive then?"

Al sputtered. "How would I—"

"You've seen photos, haven't you?" Joan pointed out. "Try to picture her at the peak of her flowering womanhood. Youthful and vivacious, that sort of thing." She waited, watching him closely. "Any desire to pursue a sexual relationship with a younger version of your grandmother?"

"This is preposterous!" Al told her.

"Yes or no, please," Joan said curtly, growing worried that lunchtime was receding rather than growing closer.

"No," Al said. "I do not have any desire whatsoever to engage in sexual activity with my grandmother!"

Joan nodded. "Good, that's a relief."

"It's outrageous!" Al tried to stand but knocked his knee against the cold metal of the table. He settled for merely sitting up a bit straighter.

She shrugged. "I had to ask, didn't I?" she said, tapping out a few more things onto her tablet.

"I don't see why you did," he huffed.

"Let's just say it's come up before." She pursed her lips and looked up from the screen. "Last one. If given the opportunity, could you resist the chance to kill Hitler?"

Al froze in consternation. Eventually he ventured, "Kill Hitler?"

Joan nodded vigorously. "If the opportunity arose, could you refrain from killing Hitler?"

"I haven't really thought about it."

"Think about it now," she said, hurrying him along. "Imagine baby Hitler, in his crib, before he's done all his Hitler things."

"Baby Hitler?" Aloysius asked. Despite himself, he could just about picture the little scamp. But why would a baby have a mustache?

"Yes." Joan leaned closer. "Would you be able to stop yourself from murdering baby Hitler?"

"I wouldn't murder any babies!" he protested, finally standing despite nearly knocking the table over.

"Even baby Hitler?" she pressed.

"Even him," Al said resolutely.

"Close enough." Another satisfied tap on the screen of her tablet. "That's it."

"What's it?" Al inquired.

"That's the end of the questionnaire." Joan began to collect her papers. "It's time to go," she added, avoiding his gaze.

"I'm not going anywhere until someone tells me what's going on," said Al, putting his foot down. Unfortunately, he was so off-balance to begin with that he nearly fell to the floor. "Just tell me, without any more nonsense: Am I dead?"

4

A YELLOWISH BEIGE

Joan sighed, straightened her papers, and considered her terrible luck. No matter who occupied the chair across from her, the conversation eventually came down to an existential crisis. And usually just before lunch.

Why? Joan asked herself. *Why me?*

"It's complicated," she said to the sweating, panicked man before her.

"How can it be complicated?" Al demanded. "Am I dead? Yes or no. It's binary."

"You're alive," Joan assured him. "Now." She shrugged. "But technically you did die."

"Then how am I alive?" Al asked.

Joan stared at a blank spot on the wall and wished they had let her put up a poster. A visual aid was so helpful for these things. "We sent an extraction team to the moment just prior to your death. The extraction team saved you and brought you back to The Institute at the Beginning of Time, leaving no one the wiser."

"Nobody noticed my body wasn't there?"

"Our team sedated you, and replaced you with a lifeless duplicate."

"You replaced me with a clone?" Al asked in horror.

Joan gestured dismissively. "A rapidly grown duplicate that was never technically alive."

"A dead clone," Al insisted.

"If you want. In the original timeline you were killed. By replacing you with a replicated double—"

"The dead clone . . ."

Joan sighed. If only she'd had a poster to show him. She pressed on. "We're not monsters. There's no suffering."

Al looked around incredulously. "I'd say I'm suffering now."

Long familiar with hardship, Joan brushed this feeble complaint aside. "All that we do here at The Institute is to preserve the integrity of space-time. Think of it this way: Everyone you once knew believes that you've died. Everything appears just as it was recorded in the history books."

That was something. "I was in the history books?"

"It's just an expression." She shook her head. "You weren't notable or influential."

"Oh, that's very nice. And just who the hell do you

think you are?" For a moment, he could have sworn she was going to sock him.

Instead, she pointed to her name tag. "I'm Joan," she said.

Al gestured for her to continue. "Just Joan?"

"Just Joan." She carefully placed the papers into a manila folder.

"Like Prince, or Madonna," Al mused.

"Not at all like the Madonna," Joan said with a strange urgency. She pressed her lips together 'til they turned white.

"But you are in show business?" he asked her, so far down the wrong track he'd have to pass through customs on his way back.

She shook her head again. "I'm afraid I've left you with a misapprehension."

"At least I'm getting something. Usually I haven't got a clue, or I have no dignity or whatever it is. I'll take getting a misapprehension over that any day."

Joan sighed and put her fingers to her temples. She could feel the headache coming. "I'm Joan of Arc."

Al snorted. "And I'm Napoléon Bonaparte."

Joan frowned. "That's not what my records show." She opened the manila folder and began to sift through her papers. "Has there been some mistake?"

"I'm not Napoléon Bonaparte," Al told her.

Relief suffused her face. "That's good." She closed the folder. "That would have meant a lot more forms."

"And I don't believe you're Joan of Arc." He pointed an accusatory finger.

"Why would I lie about it?" The charming moue returned to her face.

"Well. She's famous, isn't she?"

"Famous for dying a virgin," Joan noted wryly. "And losing a battle, right? Not to mention being captured, tried for heresy, and burned at the stake. Why would anyone want to claim that legacy?"

"Dying a virgin might not be particularly glamorous," Al admitted. "But—"

"Might I suggest you get dressed before you go any further?" Joan said. "My records indicate you'll be more comfortable clothed."

Even though the indignity of it galled him, now that it had been brought to his attention Aloysius had no choice but to acknowledge that he was naked. How that fact had escaped him so far, he wasn't quite sure. But now that he'd noticed it, he found his state of undress even more unsettling than the questions. At least it provided a reasonable explanation for his lack of pockets.

"Where are my clothes?"

"I believe your dead clone has them," Joan said wryly.

"What am I supposed to . . ."

"There's a uniform on the table." Joan kept her eyes

averted, as if she hadn't been taking notes while his naked body roasted under the lights.

"Well," Al told her. "Turn all the way around."

He pulled a neatly folded garment from the table. Seeing nowhere to go that offered privacy, he shook out the unitard and began to pull it on where he stood. At least the fabric was soft, although the cut did little for his figure. Still, it was far more flattering than having his parts dangling about and his back hair bristling every which way.

"All the way around," he reminded her.

Al examined the uniform as he put it on. It was smooth. But more than that, it was yellow. And it wasn't just any yellow. It was mildly, inoffensively yellow. It was a yellow so adulterated with blandness that it was really almost a tan. It was the kind of color that one forgets is even a color.

Before he could ask Joan for help with the unitard's zipper, it cinched itself up on its own. Although the zipper's assertive manner was a bit alarming, Aloysius was very pleased to note that he now had pockets.

"You can turn back around."

Joan turned warily, appearing to be greatly relieved at the change in decor. "Booties, too," she said, gesturing to the lumps of fabric on the table.

Al pulled on the moccasin-like footwear, feeling like nothing so much as a hospital patient waiting for surgery.

The booties tightened over his feet, the soles hardening as he gingerly tested his weight.

"And the Almanac." Joan gestured at a final limp strip of fabric still sitting on the table. "It goes around your wrist."

"Arm-anac?" He looked at the yellow band warily.

"Almanac," she said. *"The Everyday Timekeeper's Almanac."*

"Almanac? Almanac . . ." he muttered. Aloysius would have called the thin strap a bracelet, not an almanac, but that was the least of the strange oddities he'd been asked to accept. He placed the band around his wrist and was only slightly surprised to find it tightening to a comfortable fit.

"There, that's not so bad." Joan looked at him appraisingly. She dusted off his shoulders and nodded reassuringly. She was just grateful she could finally avoid the sight of his dangling bits.

Joan's proximity gave Aloysius ample time for a closer look at his interrogator. Above her name tag was a dark and frowning face with arresting brown eyes. She was wearing a yellowish-beige uniform like the one he had just put on, only she looked comfortable in it. It was the sort of thing a mental patient would wear. Was she a patient, too? Had he just been given the nth degree by a mental patient?

Suddenly dizzy, Aloysius took long, measured breaths to marshal his resources and center himself. In. Out. In . . .

"Take it easy," Joan murmured encouragingly. One

more heart attack during onboarding, and it would be back to HR for her.

Al didn't enjoy the disorientation for long before reality hit him. A platoon of questions stormed back into his consciousness, and before another second could pass, Al's voice charged from his throat. "Where am I?"

"You're—"

"And what's with all the questions about my Gram-gram?" He banged his hand on the table. "And Hitler! Really? Those were terrible questions."

Joan threw up her hands. "I don't pick the questions."

"And if you're Joan of Arc," he said shrewdly, "how is it that I can understand you? Do you really speak twenty-first-century English?"

"No, the Almanac is modulating your brainwaves to help you recognize the intent of my words while modifying your speech patterns for my benefit. In theory, misunder-standings are nearly impossible when one of the parties is using an Almanac."

Al blinked. If what she said was true, it was an amazing achievement. He gazed in wonder at the miracu-lous wristband before looking back to Joan. "What?"

"The Almanac." She pointed at his wrist, then at a bracelet on her own arm.

"The bracelet?" He reexamined the formfitting device strapped to his forearm.

"The Almanac is a personal time machine, an

omnichronal translator, and a proto-historical databank accurate to the sixth degree," Joan explained eagerly. "It's been quantum entangled with a pocket universe outside of normal space-time." It did sound impressive.

"It looks like a charity wristband," Al noted.

Joan scrunched up her face. "It is not the Almanac's purpose to look good."

"It's doing a wonderful job then."

"And any perceived shortcomings in the Almanac," Joan continued, her expression darkening, "are your own fault as much as anyone else's."

"My fault?" Al croaked.

"You're one of the Almanac's authors."

"I don't remember writing any *Everyday Timekeeper's Almanac*. It seems like the kind of thing I would remember." To be fair, Al didn't remember writing any poems dedicated to his mother, either, and there were quite a few of those on her fridge.

"It contains all the answers you'll ever need," Joan told him. "You're going to want to study it very closely."

"Closely?" he asked. "It's already on my wrist."

"You'll need to familiarize yourself with the content before you begin to contribute."

Al sneered. "You don't really expect me to believe that I'm going to write this thing?"

"Not alone." Joan said. "Many people have added to its store of knowledge, over a great span of time. It will be your

duty to contribute your own research. It's an honor, really."
She began once again to pack up her papers. "Come on. We've
got to get started on our mission before you begin to acclimate."

"Our mission?" Al prompted.

Joan nodded, happy to see lunchtime approaching
once again. "Yes. You were recruited for a specific
purpose."

Al looked wary. He massaged the wrist holding the
Almanac as if it were an old and stubborn wound. "What
purpose?"

"It's very important," Joan assured him. "We need a
local expert to help our insertion team successfully interact
with people from the . . . the residents of the . . ." She
started to flip through the papers in her manila folder.

"The early twenty-first century," Al supplied.

Joan closed the folder. "That's right."

"In Oakland."

She shook her head. "Not Oakland. Nearby, in a very
similar location . . . Fresno," Joan said.

"Fresno?" Al blurted incredulously. "Fresno's nothing
like Oakland."

Again Joan turned to her notes. "Are you sure? They're
similarly sized urban centers with the same dominant
language, less than two hundred miles away from each
other, and within the same nation state." She smiled.
"Sounds pretty similar to me."

Al harrumphed. "There are a few differences between Oakland and Fresno," he said.

"Of course there are. And you already know all about them, right?" she asked.

Al slowly nodded. "Some."

"That's why you're here," she said cheerfully. "And it's absolutely vital that you retain your twenty-first-century instincts and social conditioning, so that you can help the rest of our team blend in seamlessly. The longer you spend at The Institute, the more you'll lose your natural responses."

"I'm afraid you're suffering from a delusion," Al declared.

"I'm not delusional—"

"And since you are delusional, quite possibly dangerously so, I'm certainly not going to cooperate with you."

"It's no delusion," Joan repeated. She pressed the button beside the window. In an instant the wall grew transparent, restoring the view of the carnosaur on the hillside, now in the process of messily disgorging some bony plates.

Al shuddered. She'd made her point.

"And there are two reasons you should cooperate," Joan continued, opaquing the window with a touch. "First, to protect the integrity of the space-time continuum. And second, because if you don't help us, we'll take you back to the moment of your death and replace the replicated corpse with you."

Al winced. "That's not much of a choice," he said.

"It isn't meant to be."

He gripped the edge of the table and nodded to himself. "So, my job is . . .?"

"Just to be yourself," Joan assured him. "We may need a bit of help dealing with the locals. Just be yourself and help the rest of us appear a bit more like you."

Al looked closely, but he could detect no sarcasm. Being himself would be a new strategy for Al, but he might as well give it a try if everybody else was doing it.

"And what will the rest of you be doing?" he asked.

"We're going back to protect the timeline," Joan said with determination. "To prevent an unauthorized alteration in the recorded course of history."

"Alteration?" Al asked.

"When a rogue time traveler begins to alter the timeline—"

"Rogue time traveler?"

"Whoever's responsible for the illegal revision," Joan explained. "We're able to sense a polychronal flux of ionized antimatter before the causality cascade reaches us. It's not exact, but we're able to locate the flux signature and derive a space-time position."

"I've heard of that," Al said. "But I don't think I've seen it done."

Joan went on as if he hadn't spoken. "The nexus for this incursion appears to be at the Byers Arena in Fresno," she informed him, "a little over two years after your death."

"The Byers Arena . . ." Al shook his head.

"Are you familiar with the location?"

"An arena in Fresno? Can't say I've been. But in a place like Fresno, I'm sure they use it for beauty pageants, and monster truck rallies, and whatever. Too hot outside for that kind of thing."

Joan looked back at her notes. "We believe there was a 'med convention' at the arena on the day in question," she read. "It led to what we consider a vital historical event."

"A bunch of doctors in suits networking in an air-conditioned arena? I don't see how that's a vital historical event."

"Readings of this magnitude aren't ambiguous," she informed him coolly.

"It's just hard to imagine."

"We don't believe it was the convention itself that was a vital historical event," she went on, "only the bombing."

That had his attention. "A bombing? In Fresno? Who would bomb Fresno?"

"Something called a 'domestic terrorist cell'."

"So, we're going back to stop this bombing from . . ."

Joan sighed loudly. "Haven't you been listening to a word I've said?"

"Most of them," Al assured her.

"We're protecting the timeline."

"You mean . . ."

"We need to make sure events occur exactly as they were recorded in the historical database. In this case, that event was a bombing."

"That's . . . monstrous," Al said, his neurons sputtering like a stalling engine.

"We protect the timeline." Her tone was firm.

"Protect the timeline," Al said in distaste. "You want me to help you blow up Fresno."

"Don't be dramatic; we only want you to help blow up the arena. Just over a hundred people are killed." Joan had just enough sensitivity to notice Al's discomfort. "It's a tragedy, I know, but it's already happened. And we're not the ones who did it."

"It's monstrous," he said again.

Joan cleared her throat judiciously. "It is. But it's not our place to impose our moral judgments on the course of history. If we did—if we tried to alter history for the better —the consequences could be catastrophic. Humanity itself might be lost. With those stakes, our squeamishness is immaterial. Our objections don't matter. It's the timeline that matters." Joan stood a bit straighter. "The timeline must be preserved. And we're going to do it."

"And you're the good guys?" Al clarified.

Joan rolled her eyes. "Of course, *we're* the good guys. You're a good guy now too."

"But—"

"Oh, how the time slips away. No more questions," Joan told him, trying to sound sympathetic. "You've got to meet the rest of the team."

"Where are we going?" Al couldn't even find the room's exit.

"I'm staying here," Joan informed him. "You're going to the lab."

"What lab?"

"You'll see," she said, most of her attention shifting to the contents of her manila folder. "Follow the yellow arrows in the corridor until you reach the lab. The rest of the team is already there."

A door opened itself before them like the pupil of a great eye dilating, until it was large enough to engulf him. Al had the uncomfortable feeling that he stood facing a giant birth canal. He hesitated, too embarrassed to admit how much the prospect of walking away from this near-stranger terrified him. Regardless, a large part of him wanted to weep, and beat his chest, and generally throw himself on her mercy. He settled on a disappointed "huh."

Joan gave him a light shove toward the door. "Follow the yellow arrows, and you'll be there in no time," she said, her eyes glued to her tablet.

Follow the yellow arrows. Al was glad for such a simple instruction. He was beginning to feel doom wasn't quite as imminent. He turned back to Joan, intent on asking one or two last questions. "Is this—"

"Why don't you refer to the Almanac?" Joan said, rubbing her forehead. "For now, just speak into your wristband. At least until it grows familiar with your thought patterns."

Al looked down at the tight-fitting contraption strapped to his arm. He was still staring blankly at the device as Joan ushered him to the door.

"It's the last step of the onboarding process," Joan said from behind him. "Here." She grabbed his hand and pulled his wrist to her mouth. "External Override. Retrieve entry: 'The Grandmother Corollary'."

And with a firm but gentle push, Joan propelled him into the unknown.

5

THE ARROW

AL STOOD IN A BRIGHT, spartan corridor, curved just enough that no end could be seen. The door had barely contracted back to a blank wall behind him when a calm and mellifluous voice spoke. It didn't seem to be originating from the Almanac, but rather from somewhere inside Al's head. Reeling, he tried to focus on the words. This was somewhat difficult. Not only were the words coming from within his own mind but taken together they formed decidedly unsettling sentences.

"A special case of the Predestination Paradox, the Grandmother Corollary is the time-loop created when a timekeeper goes back in time and becomes intimate with his own grandmother. The timekeeper in question risks becoming his own grandfa-

*ther, and probably quite nauseated in any case. See
entries for 'Stable Time-Loop,' 'Multiverse Theory,'
and 'Psychiatric Counseling Services'."*

It wasn't the voice in and of itself that troubled him; Aloysius was perfectly used to hearing voices in his head. In fact, a particularly obnoxious resident harangued him with questions like, *"Is that really what you're wearing?"* and, *"Are you sure no one noticed you doing that?"* There was also a visitor with a gentle, reassuring voice. *"Just do it,"* the kind voice would urge him. Or else it would tell him, *"You deserve a break today,"* without any meaningful discrimination.

This was an entirely new voice. An unfamiliar voice. A voice that didn't belong there.

The strange and novel monologue made Al more than a little uneasy. The voice did have a soothing tone, but it peppered its lengthy explanations with phrases that Aloysius couldn't properly define, like "recursive causal loop" and "Novikov self-consistency principle." It just wasn't the sort of thing that the usual voices would say. Not that he was a fan of the usual voices—some of them had a tendency to be a bit abrasive—but over the course of twenty-something years of living with them in his head, he'd grown used to their company.

Yet whenever Aloysius so much as mumbled, this voice

would respond. It had begun to happen even if he merely thought something loudly. The most recent mistake Aloysius had made was to wonder to himself, "Where the hell am I?" which that infernal voice took as an invitation to regale him at length.

"Welcome to The Institute at the Beginning of Time. Located on the southern tip of South America in the late Cretaceous period, The Institute is a classic example of brutalist architecture. Eschewing aesthetics in favor of utilitarian design, The Institute is famous for completely failing to achieve either of those ideals. At least it would be famous, if anyone other than The Institute's staff even knew it existed. You are currently walking in Section 2B of The Institute's Grand Pedestrian Concourse, a dynamic and unmapped network of corridors connecting all main working departments."

It's not hard to see Aloysius' problem, and why he vastly preferred looking for the next yellow arrow to listening to this mystifying monologue. They were reassuring, squat little arrows with gently curling tails and an extra pair of nubs sticking out the side. The yellow arrows were easy to find, on a panel every few yards alongside a handful of symbols like green leaves, blue diamonds, and red circles. *Who in the world would come up with something like that?*

"*Professor Edward Filigree founded The Institute at the Beginning of Time soon after inventing the world's first working time machine. Actually, it was founded quite a long time before the invention of the world's first working time machine—but not from the perspective of Professor Filigree.*"

The perspective of Professor Filigree seemed to be rather all-encompassing, given the portraits, prints, and pictures of the man hanging along The Institute's corridors. Al rested his gaze on a nearby painting. Professor Filigree had a narrow face and a sharp chin. He wore wire-framed spectacles above his beak of a nose and below his close-cropped hair. In every portrait, he had the same tolerant and bemused smile—halfway to a smirk. In Al's estimation it was a rather unremarkable sort of face, the kind that always felt familiar.

"After recruiting a team of like-minded scientists and engineers, Professor Filigree and the progenitors of The Institute decided to build their headquarters in the late Cretaceous, a period they judged would be free of the meddling of other time travelers."

Al passed another genial portrait of Professor Filigree. In each painting and photo, his elaborate costume was wildly different, but his expression of benevolent wisdom remained the same. The professor's face looked down from every surface: Here was Professor Filigree smiling in a red beret; there, he was smiling in an elaborate blue-blouse-and-cravat combo; and down the hall, Professor Filigree was smiling in some sort of silver spacesuit. The voice continued:

"In this, as in many things, the progenitors were completely, stupendously, and tragically wrong. See entries for 'Unexpected Alterations to the Timeline,' 'How to Dominate Your Doppelgänger,' and 'The Big No-No (And Why Not!)'."

An avalanche of questions tumbled into Al's consciousness. Immediately he did his very best to avoid thinking overly much, especially about any questions that might trigger a response from the gentle voice. He soon learned that it was surprisingly difficult to just shut off one's brain completely, no matter how easy it looked on TV. It was a bit like telling oneself not to think of an elephant in a tutu. One soon found they couldn't help but picture an elephant in a tutu, right down to the pink frill. The more Aloysius tried to silence his thoughts, the louder they clamored. It all came to a head again, to his head in particular, when he passed a large room with furniture hanging from the ceiling and off-putting abstract art nailed to the walls.

"On your left is the former location of the Department of Paradox Avoidance (DPA), created in order to prevent the sort of time-traveling paradox that would cause space-time to fold in on itself like a poorly constructed origami crane, quite possibly destroying the multiverse in the process. Unfortunately, the DPA itself disappeared an undetermined length of time ago.

"Professor Filigree himself once said, 'There but for the DPA goes The Institute, and soon after all the rest of it.' It's hard to overstate the impor-

*tance of the DPA. Despite the department's myste-
rious absence, The Institute's layout remains
unaltered, in the hopes that the DPA may soon
return. In fact, it may have been there all along.
Frankly, it could be the case that we've simply
forgotten to check on it, which would certainly be
embarrassing, but not nearly so tragic as the deaths
of the hundreds of Institute researchers and timekeepers hard at work in the DPA. If they were ever
there in the first place."*

Aloysius busied himself looking for yellow arrows and
let his feet do their own thinking. With every step, he tried
to clear his mind of meaningless patter, to focus only on
the present moment. If Aloysius had been more spiritually
inclined, he might have recognized that he was performing
a sort of circumambulation—a walking meditation—setting
aside the mundane and opening his mind to the sacred. In
this instance, there was nothing less likely than a revela-
tion: Aloysius was exactly as spiritual as a brick, and just
about as dense.

He did recognize the feeling, eventually, as something
similar to his mood after playing four or five hours of
Tetris, when he would fall asleep dreaming of spinning,
falling tetrominoes. It wasn't a good feeling. Not exactly. It
was as if he were no longer experiencing the passage of

time or space, all of it swept away in the flow of his subconscious mind.

At least that damn voice wasn't intruding, not for the last few steps. Which made him wonder why it had spoken to him in the first place.

"The Everyday Timekeeper's Almanac *is a compendium of knowledge that transcends the normal boundaries of space-time. Compiled by the infinite researchers of The Institute across an infinite multiverse of possibilities, the Almanac contains every fact and every theory that any Institute recruit thought might prove useful to their fellow timekeepers.*

"*Presumably, a timekeeper somewhen discovered how to store the Almanac's databanks in a causally isolated pocket universe, accessible from any point in space-time. Remember, no matter when or where you go, the Almanac's just a thought away.*

"*As a new recruit, you will eventually be expected to add your own store of knowledge to* The Everyday Timekeeper's Almanac. *Or you may have already done so. Regardless, you almost certainly will have already done so at some point. Just take it as a given, all right?*"

But it wasn't all right. None of it was all right. He'd been shot in the head, he was alone and lost in a maze of corridors, and his charity wristband was telepathically communicating with him. This was the moment when Al looked back on his earlier confusion with fondness and longing. Aloysius would have given away his right arm if it meant he could be naked and watching the dinosaurs again.

And what's worse, he was all out of yellow arrows.

Just as Aloysius began to formulate the thought, "Where to now?" and prompt that disarming voice again, a shiny metal door opened. Al could have sworn that it hadn't been a door the first time he'd looked. Before it opened, there had been no hint of *door-ness* at all. It had seemed just another shiny stretch of hallway.

6

CLINK AND CRANK

Relieved to have any lingering remnant of personal autonomy dismissed, Aloysius walked through the portal with the same lack of caution as a cow patiently queuing in the slaughterhouse chute. This particular portal revealed two forms standing at a workbench in a cluttered room. Though they were only a few yards away, neither reacted to Al's entrance.

One of them, a small and slender man, had loose servo-mechanisms and trailing wire conduits at the shoulder where an arm should be. Gears and servos could be seen squiggling around from the joint. When the man turned his head, Al could have sworn he saw a USB port in the back of his neck. To make things even more absurd, the mechanical monstrosity was wearing a preposterously large red helmet and fiddling with a detached limb. He appeared to be enjoying himself, if the satisfied grunting could be trusted to convey the mood of a . . . whatever he was. A robot? An android?

The other figure at the workbench was the most intimidating nun that Al had ever seen, which was saying quite a lot, since he'd spent one memorable year at a Catholic school run by The Sisters of Delayed Gratification. But the woman was more severe than any teacher, and more weathered than any farmer. She was lean, not an iota of excess mass on her body. She stood like a coiled spring ready to explode. With her right hand, she used a small metal tool to tinker with gleaming machinery scattered on the workbench. In her left hand, she held a roasted chicken drumstick. It smelled quite good.

Seeing Al, the woman scowled.

Al opened his mouth to speak, but the woman held up a finger to forestall him, somehow without letting go of either chicken or tool. It took an impressive will to stymie Al when roasted chicken was involved, but the woman wasted no more time on the effort and turned back to her meal. Al stood in silence, watching as every ounce of matter was sucked from the bone and into her ravenous maw.

Al hadn't planned on actually waiting for her to finish eating before he spoke, but it took all of twenty seconds for the strange woman to polish off the drumstick. He felt sure that if he'd accidentally rested his hand too close, she would have taken a bite of his finger and swallowed without a care for his screams. By the end of the performance Al's disgust had turned into fear, and then his fear into a fascinated awe. What kind of bleak dystopian pit had spawned this barbarian? Clearly, she'd been raised before flatware had been *en vogue*.

The appalling woman stood, revealing her long black habit. Above it, the giant began adjusting a wimple on her head. When she was satisfied, she slowly spun in a circle with her arms outstretched.

"And?" she asked after she'd come back around. "How do we look?"

Al struggled between honesty and diplomacy for a moment. "I'm sorry?" he asked, playing for time.

"How do we look in the uniforms?" She gestured at her nun's habit.

"That?"

"To blend in with the idiots," she explained to her dimwitted pupil.

"Blend in? Wearing that?" Despite the success of his conversational gambit, Al could tell some kind of declarative sentence was going to be required of him soon.

She looked back to see her companion ignoring their conversation. "Hang on," she told Al. "He's not doing it right." She was frowning, but the mechanical man paid her no heed.

"I'm Al," Al declared, feeling that he'd found some solid ground on which to make his stand.

"Impala," she said. "Joan send you?"

"She told me to follow the yellow arrows, and I haven't seen her since." He peered into the corners of the crowded room: mysterious machinery, unfamiliar weaponry, and the carcasses of an enormous number of chickens. "Am I in the right place?"

"Did you follow the yellow arrows?" Impala asked pointedly.

"Yes."

"Then you're in the right place."

Reluctantly, Al stepped away from the door. It promptly closed behind him with the finality of a trap snapping shut. "What are all the other colors for?"

"What colors?"

Al gestured vaguely to where the doorway had once led to the hall. "Blue diamonds, red circles—"

"Those." Impala nodded. "They lead where you don't want to go," she said, examining him more closely. "You're not quite as ugly as I would have expected."

Al was fairly certain she didn't intend to eat him, but her smile was frightening, nonetheless. *Time to try some of that patented charm,* one of the old and familiar voices told Al in his head. *Best to make friends before she decides you'd make a good dessert.* "So . . ." he started, with nowhere to go. "Where are you from?" He aimed an ingratiating smile at her but failed to acquire a target.

Impala slowly licked each of her fingers, staring at him

with naked contempt. Al considered the possibility that the translator wasn't working properly. He had just resolved to forget the whole thing when a belch traveled from Impala's belly to her mouth and echoed through the lab.

"I was born in Cleveland," she said mournfully.

"Cleveland?" He was amazed. "*Cleveland*, really?"

"You've been?" She cocked her head at him like a wary predator.

"I've never had the pleasure," Al said.

The mechanical man turned his head to face them. "When," he prompted. It wasn't just the first thing he'd said to Al, it was the first acknowledgement of any kind he'd made that Al had walked into the room.

Al knew this was his chance for a good first impression. He searched desperately for a clever quip. He had something queued up about the toy robot he'd been given for his sixth birthday, but suddenly it didn't seem like the right time. *Say something*, he urged himself. *Say something insightful*. "When?" Al asked. "When what?"

Impala snickered.

"When are you from," the machine repeated. "*When* is the better question."

"Of course." Al turned back to the savage. "When are you from?"

Impala narrowed her eyes. "I was born forty winters after The Fall."

Aloysius struggled mightily to leap across this chasm of understanding and came up lamentably short. "Winter's always after fall," he said, clinging to the metaphorical precipice.

"Not 'fall'," Impala insisted. "*The* Fall."

"I think you can say it either way," Al told her. "Or 'autumn,' though that's a bit more . . . a bit more . . . I don't know, poetical."

"The Fall of Humanity," she clarified.

"Oh," Al said, feigning an epiphany. "Of course. I see." He certainly didn't, but a lifetime of social conditioning left Al making a great many meaningless statements. If he'd been at a cocktail party, he would have left the matter there, and gone to look for some cheese, or a canapé. With no toothpick-friendly appetizers in sight, he decided to focus on nodding agreeably.

"Twenty-third century in the Gregorian calendar," the mechanical man said, taking pity on him. "Famine, collapse of social structures, displacement and death of billions."

"Ah," Al said, frowning politely. "Sounds rough." Al felt rather upset at the prospect; it was disheartening to think humanity could fall so low, even if it was only Cleveland. What could have done it? How could it have happened? "I should have known it would happen in Cleveland," Al mused aloud.

Impala hissed through clenched teeth. "How could

you have known?" she asked him with palpable hostility. "Were you there? Did you have something to do with it?" The thick muscles on her neck had tensed, and a vein on her forehead enlarged considerably.

Al's muscles, already feeling quite put out, fled deeper into the surrounding tissue. Barely keeping his head up, he mumbled, "Just a joke."

"A joke?" Impala snarled at him.

Al held his hands out, palms up. "I wasn't serious," he said, his outstretched hands beginning to quiver.

"It wasn't funny." She was livid. "Are all of the before-timers this stupid?" she asked. "They must have been. I grew up in the hell you created, asshole. Do you have any idea what you people did to the planet? You poisoned the globe with your greed and madness. Even your waste lasted for eons."

"Not funny," Al said. "Gotcha." He didn't have a clue what had upset her.

Impala, on the other hand, relived that nightmare each time she closed her eyes.

7

WHITTLING CAMINO

IMPALA WAS FROM CLEVELAND. But more to the point, she was from the back seat of a Chevy Trailblazer. At that juncture the car had long since lost any pretension of vehicular status. By then it sat more or less permanently on the shoulder of a great concrete path, just south of a bridge over one of the caustic rivers feeding the fetid waters of Lake Erie.

There's nothing particularly unusual about being born in a midsize sport utility vehicle. Over the centuries there have been a great number of childbirths on the back seats of automobiles, and more than a few conceptions. But Impala's birth didn't occur during a hectic drive to the local hospital, or while her parents were hunkered down and stranded by a terrible storm. Like most children of the twenty-third century, she was born in the family home.

Impala's family lived in that rusted, rotted husk of an

SUV, and they felt lucky to have it. After all, the Trailblazer had seven seats, and there were only six of them. The roof leaked in the heavy rains, but they'd grown used to the smell of mildew and rot. Most important, by far, was that it kept out the wolves. There were a lot of wolves. By the mid-twenty-third century, there were exponentially more wolves lurking around than functioning coffee shops.

Despite the surfeit of wolves, Impala didn't like to think of herself as prey. That's why she spent so many long days learning to become a predator. She caked herself in mud to cover the human scent of her. She walked slowly upwind, to come upon her prey undetected. She made her own weapons out of salvaged steel and the sinew of her kills. She didn't trust anyone other than one brother and two sisters. The rest of them, even her parents, were useless. Worse than useless, really—they were a liability.

Impala knew a great deal about liabilities. Not in the sense of insurance, which was rather hard to obtain in the post-apocalyptic hellscape she called home, but in the way that an undisciplined companion could bring down disaster upon even the most careful of hunters. Her mother and father had been a burden. Raised by Impala's long-dead grandparents, her parents had grown up hearing stories of the time before—the long, long ago. They were seductive stories, fantastic and alluring, and Impala was thoroughly sick of them. She suffered from no such dreams herself.

Impala and her siblings were raised by the wastelands, with only the cracked plexiglass of a Chevy Trailblazer to keep out the wind and the cold. They didn't even have secondhand memories of a time before The Fall to warm them. Her mother had told Impala there had been more humans once, a great many more, more humans than wolves even. It was hard for Impala to believe humanity had been capable of such feats; but neither could she credit the wolves for the great concrete jungles, the moldering city, or the ash and smoke that obscured the sun.

In those cyclopean ruins, Impala learned to take care of herself, to trust only her siblings, and to ignore such trivialities as comfort, hygiene, and matching socks. In point of fact, Impala had never worn matching socks even once in her life.

Her boots were made from the skin of a bear, and she padded the interiors with scraps and rags that served to keep her warm and to stave off trench foot. She had killed the bear herself, then skinned it, and in the end proved once and for all that she wouldn't get very far as a shoemaker. She wore the boots anyway and experienced a perverse pleasure when given the opportunity to show them off.

In stark contrast to her meager wardrobe, her armory was bursting. Impala even had a gun—there were an awful lot of them just lying around growing rusty—but working ammunition was unheard of. Which was remarkable really, considering that at one point there were thousands of cartridges for every gun. The cartridges had lasted only slightly longer than the coffee shops. She had an old shotgun herself, with a barrel that was smooth and narrow and useful for straightening arrows.

When Impala's parents inevitably died—her father eaten by a pack of feral schnauzers, her mother succumbing to complications from an ingrown tocnail—Impala and her siblings continued on without much notice. The only appreciable difference was that the four of them had quite a bit more room in the Trailblazer, and Impala no longer felt encumbered by her father's blundering help on her hunts.

Among the scattered survivors of Cleveland, one of the last bastions of humanity on the continent, Impala had become a renowned hunter. It was a position that left her not well respected exactly, but well avoided. In a way, it was strange that the people of Cleveland would avoid her; Impala was useful and reliable. She almost never returned to the family Trailblazer empty-handed, whether that meant a buck over her shoulder, some hares hanging from her belt, or a choice piece of salvage from the dismal ruins of the city proper.

But Impala was dangerous. Dangerous to the wolves, dangerous to her rivals, dangerous even to well-wishers who came close without announcing themselves loudly and waving their arms about first. So Impala scavenged alone on the shores of Lake Erie, with only the howls of an overbold wolf or two to keep her company.

On one particularly successful salvaging trip, she returned to the Trailblazer with a can opener. Though none of her family had ever seen a sealed can, the object was still a marvel. The gears spun with such precision when one turned the handle. Soon, Impala gave the can opener to her little brother Camino. He'd used it to whittle, which was just about the only form of entertainment left to them.

His sisters called him Whittling Camino, on account of his great love for the craft. Their parents had given him the Camino part of the name. None of them knew just what Camino meant, but it was a family name, and tradition was important. Somehow, it became even more important as the structures of society crumbled, and the very concept of civilization was forgotten.

Whittling Camino would sit on the hood of the Trailblazer and whittle, usually with a small pocketknife, but sometimes with the can opener, which he would use to score grooves. It was, all in all, an uneventful sort of existence. It wasn't that Camino didn't get out enough, although he surely didn't. It was simply that there wasn't much to get into or out of in the first place.

Camino made his own entertainment. He whittled. He crafted fantastic images, and created the only toys the children of House Chevrolet had ever known. He carved a likeness of Impala's face onto a wooden mug and put a howling wolf on the haft of her axe.

It was a real talent that Whittling Camino had, but it didn't do much to help them gather food or the supplies necessary for their family to survive the increasingly harsh winters. Those tasks were left to Impala and her two sisters, who scoured the surrounds every day from dawn to dusk, occasionally trading with other survivors, more frequently scavenging from the dilapidated shelters of the most recent casualties.

When the Chevrolet sisters each returned with their various finds, Camino would exclaim appreciatively. Then, predictable as always, he would offer up his latest carving to trade to the neighbors. The sisters would exclaim over the fantastic shapes, the intricate details, the lifelike vivacity, and invariably, they would tell him to keep the carvings, because they were too beautiful and unique to trade away for mere necessities like food and tools.

They really were a rather kind group of sisters, because in reality no one wanted any more of Whittling Camino's work. Every hovel and cave, every burnt-out car and crumbling motor home within a day's hike was already adorned with a leaping trout carved from an old log, or a nicely detailed doorstop. They hadn't the heart to tell Camino how worthless his trinkets had become. When the entire pool of customers consists of the hundred or so survivors they could find in a ten-mile radius, market saturation was a very real and very powerful force.

Camino filled the Trailblazer with ornaments until the car grew so crowded that he began to pile up his creations outside the wreck. Soon, the toppling towers threatened to engulf the Trailblazer. More than once, Impala found herself kicking her way through a stack of wooden trinkets as if it were an errant snowbank. When she realized what she was doing, she'd turn guiltily to glance back at their home. Then she would far more carefully trudge through the debris, staying on the well-worn paths winding between the heaps of Camino's treasures.

The sisters were so consistently kind to Camino, so understanding of his artist's temperament and his utter lack of pragmatism and perspective, that Camino believed —really, truly believed—that he was a contributing and useful member of the family.

Their youngest sister, Corsica, had taken to squealing with delight each time Camino presented her with a detailed owl figurine, or another barely functional whistle. Because of this, Camino gave Corsica almost all of his creations. This was a situation that Impala and Beretta were happy to tolerate, since it meant they no longer needed to feign delight as yet another themed chess set was gifted to them one piece at time.

Impala in particular had grown tired of Camino's

constant need for approval. But she was willing to follow her sisters' lead when it came to humoring him.

It came as a great surprise one spring afternoon when Camino presented Impala with something extraordinary— a wooden fishhook. The object was delicate but strong, quite sharp at the end, and even had a barb to help hold the fish. There was an eyelet that would just fit Impala's sinew line. It was practical, simple, and elegant.

It was entirely unlike Camino.

"You know," he told her as he handed it over, "for catching those slimy lake rats."

"Huh" was all Impala managed to say, so busy was she examining the marvelous creation.

"Huh," Impala grunted after she pricked her finger on the remarkable tip.

"Huh," she told Camino, thinking over the implications of this extraordinary invention.

"You could just tell me you don't like it," Camino huffed at her, so used had he grown to Corsica's ebullient praise that he didn't recognize real appreciation right before his eyes.

"No, this is"—Impala struggled for a moment to find the word—"useful," she said in wonder.

"I thought it might be," said Camino.

"And we could trade it," added Impala.

"Trade it?" Camino asked, careful not to spoil the mood. It was the most excited he'd ever seen his sister.

"Not this one," Impala added, spinning the hook in question between her fingers. "Only if you make more. Can you make more?"

"Yes, I think so."

"But I'm keeping this one."

"I . . ." Camino found himself quite lost. "Of course."

"Corsica! Beretta!" Impala called toward the Trailblazer. "Come see this."

The three sisters gathered around and quietly marveled together at Camino's creation. Each of them in turn pricked themselves on the surprisingly sharp tip. The sisters smiled at one another, and as one, they turned to him with expressions of pride. Immediately, Camino began to wonder if he was being mocked.

As is often the case with difficult artists, Camino didn't know what to do when confronted with real admiration. He had expected his oeuvre to remain unappreciated until after his death, and being only nineteen, he had a good ten or twenty more years of life ahead of him. It was in his post-mortem period that Camino anticipated the real fame would roll in. He liked to think there would be admirers from all over Northeastern Ohio, waiting to take a turn marveling at the amazing likeness of the bald eagle, the consistency of the humorously themed chess pieces, and the sheer quantity of ornamental doorstops.

Instead, Camino was very much alive, and quite a bit baffled, to find strangers arriving at the family Trailblazer hoping to trade. Within weeks, he began to receive two or even three visitors a day, each laden with goods to barter and hoping only to procure one of Whittling Camino's miraculous fishhooks. Ten beaver hides or two rusty golf clubs was the going rate, and Camino and his sisters soon looked to be getting very wealthy indeed—at least in terms of pelts and putters. Each of the siblings fashioned new winter coats, soft moccasins, and lined gloves. They even stitched together new seat covers for the Trailblazer.

It was a time of great abundance and cheer. Camino quickly grew into his role as the foremost purveyor of wooden fishing accoutrements in the Greater Cleveland area. Though Corsica and Beretta were happy just to have him pitching in, Impala found herself strangely jealous of his newfound status. She could come home at dusk with a fat doe slung over her shoulder and receive no more welcome than the days she had only a mangy squirrel. It was worse than not being appreciated, worse even than being taken for granted. She wasn't needed.

As Camino's fame grew, Impala looked for riskier and more exciting exploits, hoping for a kill so worthy that her name would be sung, or a discovery so amazing it would upend the survivors' struggling economy. But wherever she went, she found only ruins, and heard the name of Whittling Camino whispered with awe.

Three months after bearing witness to Camino's first fishhook, Impala was dead, a victim of her own ambition.

8

MANUFACTURER'S SPECIFICATIONS

IMPALA MUTTERED SOMETHING ABOUT A "DEVIL" under her breath as she turned from Al. Then she growled at the man across the table, "Get your arm back on, nimrod. You're freaking out the new recruit." The cyborg turned to Impala with a surprisingly lifelike expression of annoyance on his face. He was a convincing simulacrum of a human, even though Al had already seen behind the curtain.

The mechanical man placed his detached arm on a table littered with tools and parts that Al had no way of identifying. He scratched his forehead with his remaining hand. The detached limb made a rude gesture toward Impala.

"Another recruit." The metallic creature—whatever it was—took a long look at Al. "How unfortunate." Al had to admit it even sounded like a real person.

Plucking his arm from the table, HCL used it to scratch the small of his back.

"Aloysius Cook. Hello," Al said, holding out his hand to shake. "You can call me Al."

HCL handed him the spare arm. "Hold this."

Al examined the limb with growing unease. It was still moving.

Impala snatched the arm from Al. "Don't expect much in the way of social niceties from HCL. He's not as sensitive as I am," she said, throwing the arm at the mechanical man. He plucked it out of the air and set it gently on the workbench.

"Of course," Al said, nodding eagerly. "Because he's an android."

HCL shook his head. "I am a cyborg," he announced with great dignity.

Al raised his eyebrows. "Wow. No kidding. I'll try to remember that." He'd forgotten the term before he finished his sentence.

HCL scoffed. "It never fails. It's always right when you're about to turn on the particle accelerator." He swept his work aside. "That's when some idiot walks in."

What had they been talking about, anyway? Al wondered. They were both looking at him. Al had a peculiar tactic he'd developed for use in just such a circumstance: He'd trot out an aphorism. Since no one quite knew what the aphorism meant in the first place, they couldn't very well tell Al it didn't apply.

"A bird in the hand," Al said knowingly.

The room fell silent.

Impala and HCL simply ignored him. They considered his comment too stupid to acknowledge.

Noting their lack of argument, Al smiled inwardly. *They're going for it!*

"I told you to put the arm back on, junk heap, and don't forget the rocket hand." Impala gestured to the prototype limb on the cluttered table.

HCL picked it up and resumed using it as a backscratcher.

"Rocket hand?" Al marveled.

"Every time he leaves it behind," Impala continued, "that's when we end up . . ." Impala mimed stabbing someone in the gut, repeatedly. Eventually she sidled behind her imaginary foe and with a quick cut put them out of their misery.

"Fine," the cyborg snapped. "Just a second." After one more satisfying scratch, HCL socketed the limb into his shoulder with an audible click.

"And the hat," Impala reminded him.

"It's a helmet," HCL corrected, plucking a large red hat from beneath the table and donning what was clearly a firefighter's helmet.

"Twirl," Impala ordered.

HCL held his limbs out and slowly twirled. The cyborg was wearing a full firefighter's rig, even down to the boots.

"I apologize for the ruse," HCL stated as he came to a stop. "We are not really from the twenty-first century, ancient hominid," HCL confessed. "The confusion you're feeling is a perfectly natural response to confusing and contradictory stimuli outside the realm of your limited understanding." He grimaced with sympathy.

Al nodded. "A stitch in time," he said.

"Yes?" Impala demanded when he didn't continue. "What?"

"What?" Al asked.

"A stitch in time?" she prompted.

"Absolutely," Al agreed. "She gets it," he said in admiration.

Impala grunted with dismay. "Fine. What did you think of the uniforms?"

Al considered the six-and-a-half-foot nun and the surly firefighter with a great deal of concern. So far, they hadn't exactly established themselves as exemplars of rational behavior. Was he going to have to work with these morons? *Better get them headed in the right direction,* Al told himself. He drummed his fingers on the worktable, before finally answering. "I'm slightly concerned that the two of you won't blend in wearing those costumes."

"Costumes?" Impala scowled, looking around. "You mean the uniforms?" she asked defensively.

"Are they uniforms really?" Al pondered. "Do nuns wear uniforms?"

"They were Almanac-approved choices." Impala held up her hand to show Al the device strapped to her forearm. It was identical to his own.

"The wristwatch told you to wear that?" Al asked with suspicion.

"*The Everyday Timekeeper's Almanac*," HCL corrected, showing his forearm to Al.

"If I write that part sometime in the future, I'll apologize," Al said. Suddenly he noted Impala was staring at his jugular with more than casual interest. Al took a step back and changed the subject. "Where's my costume?"

"Uniform," Impala snarled.

"Uniform," Al agreed reluctantly.

She gestured to his torso. "You're wearing it."

"This beige thing?" Al looked down at the entirely unremarkable yellow cloth.

HCL explained, "The suit will alter its appearance automatically upon temporal transference. We're simply finalizing our designs before the temporal incursion."

"What have you got me going as?"

But Impala wasn't listening. She'd already learned that Al was a completely normal human specimen of the twenty-first century: Almost everything he said could be safely ignored without consequence. Still, the criticism had gotten to her. "You really think I don't look like a nun?" she asked.

Al waved his hands and arms about a bit, palms out to ward her off. "Who's to say what does and doesn't look like a nun nowadays?" Al gestured at HCL. "Some people might find a firefighter costume offensive. But I say, more power to him."

Impala cocked her head. "Forget the uniforms," she snorted. "Is there anything else we'll need to blend in?"

That was an easy one. "Cell phones," he told her. "We'll need cell phones."

"We can do phones," Impala said enthusiastically. "We just got back from the 1950s."

"No. Nothing like that. Those were big, old, rotary monsters." He held up his hands like he was carrying a watermelon. "We need cell phones. Little ones." He demonstrated the dimensions with his hands.

Impala, who had long ago grown used to strange voices in her head, retrieved the Almanac's entry on cell phones with a thought. The reassuring voice began at once.

"A cellular telephone is the single most important possession of any resident of the early twenty-first century. The 'cell phone' is a small, beeping, rectangular device that can be held in the hand or

stored in a pocket or tote. Such a device must be conferred with, spoken to, and tapped or prodded at regular intervals—certainly no less than every ten or fifteen minutes.

"The exact specifications of the device are entirely unimportant. If anyone expresses surprise at the appearance or function of such a device, suspicion is easily allayed by referring to the device as either 'just-released' or 'retro,' and describing its features as 'whiz-bang' or 'a bit of a letdown.' In all cases, it should frequently be stated that the time traveler wishes to procure a new device as soon as possible, one that is either bigger or smaller, louder or quieter, and generally in every way superior to the current iteration of said device.

"Great care should be taken when the time traveler must interact with another's personal cell phone. Touching someone else's device without their leave violates one of the culture's strictest taboos. It is exceedingly rare for such a device to be offered to any but family members and the closest of friends, and the occasion should be considered a great honor. Even then, it is primarily used to display pictures and videos of children and cats, which must be admired and cooed over."

"Sounds important," Impala noted with distaste. "We'll get HCL to do it." She tapped the cyborg on his shoulder.

HCL sighed. "Perhaps we can make the most of your presence, fellow hominid. Please walk us through the process of manufacturing cell phones."

Al blinked. "Manufacturing?"

"Material requirements, technical specifications and such," HCL explained.

Al took his time swallowing. "I'm not sure I'm qualified," he said.

HCL scowled with a very lifelike expression. "Your file said you were 'in tech'."

Al nodded reluctantly. Al was in tech like a sheep was in agriculture: Both of them were getting fleeced. "I'm afraid I don't really know much about cellular phones."

HCL sighed long and hard. "Perhaps I can find the specifications in the Almanac."

Al leapt at the suggestion. "Of course," he said quickly. "Just what I was thinking too."

After a brief telepathic consultation with his wristband, HCL turned back to Al. "I seem to have a detailed entry on a Miutok 27R," the cyborg said. "Will that suffice?"

Al tried to look like he was expending considerable effort on the question. He hemmed and hawed for a bit, finally asking, "Nothing with a bigger screen?"

HCL frowned. "I'm not sure—"

"No," Al said at once. "What am I saying? That'll be fine." He shrugged. "Who cares about the size of the screen? Really, it was stupid. Just a joke."

HCL turned to a terminal and began to input the parameters of the knockoff phone. "I believe I can devise something that will allow us to communicate with each other over a distance of approximately half a parsec."

Al breathed in sharply. "Half a parsec. Could you manage a whole parsec?"

Again, HCL frowned. "Undoubtedly. But it would increase the mass and energy requirements almost—"

"No, no," Al said, "just ignore me."

HCL considered the matter. "Another joke?" he asked.

Al threw up his hands. "I don't even know what a parsec is." His attempt at a charming smile only made him look like a cat getting into a tub of water, but still he held the expression.

Eventually HCL turned back to the console. "I see. Very well." He returned to work. "I'll begin the fabrication process at once. It should take approximately three minutes."

Three minutes, Al groaned to himself, feeling much like a starving man waiting for a microwave pizza. He glanced at Impala. She was picking her teeth with a discarded metal hand, muttering too quietly for him to understand. *No help from that quarter.*

Al contemplated three more minutes of small talk with

his new companion. *Couldn't be worse than an office birthday party,* he reassured himself. He groped desperately for some innocuous topic. *There's no such thing as a stupid question,* he reminded himself.

"You're really a . . . what was it . . . sideboard?" Al said.

"A cyborg," HCL said. "Approximately thirteen percent of my original organic tissue remains intact."

"Good on you," Al said, wondering just what this meant. *Which thirteen percent?* The question seemed quite important to Al, possessing as he did the full complement.

HCL nodded. "I am quite fond of my organic parts," he explained.

Al smiled. "I know just how you feel."

Suddenly HCL bristled. "I doubt that very much," he said, looking ever more piqued.

"No," Al insisted, not one to waste time reading the room. "I really do know how you feel—I love my organic parts too." He smiled as if their newfound bond was the greatest thing in the world.

HCL shuddered, disgusted. "I'm well aware of how much unaltered humans love their organic parts, particularly those located in the erogenous zone." He looked at Al with revulsion. "However, I doubt you fully comprehend my own feelings."

"Sure," Al agreed readily. He looked about him. "It takes all kinds."

HCL stared directly into Al's eyes, as if by vision alone

he could weigh a mere human's worth. "In my time, the only kinds 'it' takes are technologically enhanced cyborgs and a small subset of unaltered baseline humans kept isolated for breeding purposes." Again, the cyborg betrayed not a trace of humor.

Al grinned. He'd spent much of his youth hoping he'd one day be isolated for breeding purposes himself. "Whatever floats your boat, I guess."

HCL could barely suffer the inanity a moment longer. "Indeed. I am also capable of functioning as a flotation device in the event of a water landing."

Al's eyes stretched wide with shock. "What, really?" he asked.

"No," HCL answered, making no attempt to hide his scorn. "Given your predilection for nonsensical humor, I have decided to incorporate some trivial untruths into my conversational algorithm when I am in your presence."

Al ran that input through his biological cogitation device. "Thanks, I guess."

After a few moments of silence, HCL ventured a question. "In your opinion," he began, "would you say that my recent attempt at humor was a successful trial run?"

Al was taken aback. He struggled to adjust to HCL's display of vulnerability. "The thing of it is," Al began, "I didn't laugh." The truth lay silently before them.

HCL nodded eagerly. "I had noticed that." He scratched his shoulder socket. "I thought perhaps you had restrained your laughter because you were unaware that I was encouraging a humorous response." He looked at Al hopefully. "In the future, please feel free to laugh in my presence."

"That"—Al cleared his throat—"wasn't the problem."

HCL pursed his lips. "Perhaps you did not fully understand the context of the joke," he suggested.

"No, I got it." Al wondered if he could offend a cyborg. Either way, now wasn't the time to try.

But HCL didn't seem the least convinced that his joke could have fallen flat. "Are you cognitively impaired, delusional, or hallucinating?" he pressed.

"I wouldn't know, would I?" Al said. He smiled with the same type of satisfaction felt by a baker who'd guessed the exact moment his bread would burn.

HCL took another tack. "Could it be that you lack a normative laughter reflex?"

Al shook his head. "My humor reflexes are functioning at near capacity," Al told him proudly.

"Are you quite certain?" HCL asked. His eyes grew wide as another thought struck him. "Of course! Have you ever been diagnosed with antisocial personality disorder or a related emotional disorder?" He rubbed his hands together eagerly.

"No." Suddenly uncomfortable, Al leaned against the workbench and picked up a small cylinder. "But my best friend in third grade told me I was a bit of a jerk."

HCL perked up at once. "Interesting," he said with relish. "Indeed, very interesting. Was this friend a trained psychiatrist?"

"No. She was a sarcastic eight-year-old," Al informed him, idly twirling the cylinder in his hand.

HCL seemed to wilt. "I see. Then I am left with the possibility that my joke was, in fact, not funny." He looked imploringly at Al. "Unless you—"

"Yeah, that'd be what I'm leaning toward, myself." Looking closer at the cylinder in his hand, Al realized it was an errant cybernetic finger. He placed it back on the table gently, hoping no one had noticed.

HCL stared into the distance. "I will redouble my efforts when the opportunity arises."

"I'm looking forward to it," Al said.

"I was unaware you could look any direction other than forward," HCL said.

Al blinked. "Was that . . .?" Al stared at the cyborg's face for a moment but could find no hint of humor. Just in case, Al forced out a laugh. "Ha. Ha."

"Is that laughter?" HCL asked. "Why are you laughing?" He drew closer to Al. "Was I unintentionally humorous?"

Al frowned. "No, I was trying to be supportive . . . It doesn't matter."

HCL considered him with newfound respect. "I do

not require your support at this juncture," the cyborg said. "But I appreciate the intent."

Al grunted. "We might need to devise some sort of signal."

HCL grew inordinately excited. Nearly bouncing, he leaned closer and asked in a hushed tone, "A signal? What would this signal signify?"

"Well, when you use the signal, I would know that you're telling a joke," Al explained.

HCL leaned even closer. Al leaned in to meet him. They were very close now. Al could make out the most minute features of his remarkable artificial face. The eyelashes, the pores, the dimples—it was uncanny.

Intently, HCL whispered, "Are you capable of detecting longitudinal waves propagating through a gaseous medium with a frequency of one hundred to three hundred hertz?" He waited expectantly.

Al grimaced. "No." He hung his head. "I meant something like scratching the side of your nose to indicate that you're trying to be funny." Al brought his hand to the side of his sniffer to demonstrate.

HCL slowly pulled back. "I see. Scratching my nose would not be conducive to humorous improvisation, in my estimation."

Trying to remain hopeful, Al suggested, "We can both think about it."

"Indeed," HCL said, with no trace of his former enthusiasm.

There was a loud ding, like the timer on a child's toy oven.

Al frowned. "No, that's too obvious. Everyone will hear it."

"That was the manufacturing unit."

"Sorry?" Al said in a puzzled tone.

HCL pulled open a small door on the side of the table. "Here we are." HCL took four steaming rectangles out of a small compartment.

Al grew excited. "The cell phones are ready!" He tried to pick one up and dropped it immediately. "Why are they hot?" he asked, blowing on his fingertips.

"Heat is a byproduct of the manufacturing process."

Al nodded wisely. "And why does it smell like popcorn?" he asked.

HCL shrugged. "The lab's previous technician did not always follow the safety protocols concerning use of the molecular reorganizer."

"Oh, there's one in every office," Al put in.

"One what?" HCL asked.

Al weighed the issue a bit before settling on an answer. "One of the popcorn people," he explained. "Someone who just doesn't care that we live in a society."

HCL was unimpressed. "I fail to understand the source of your anger."

"These things are pretty culturally specific," Al said, tapping his foot idly. "If you have any other problems understanding twenty-first-century culture, be sure and let me know."

HCL grew eager. "I already have quite a few questions concerning twenty-first-century Fresno," he said happily.

Al sighed. "Okay, shoot."

HCL put down his tools and turned his full attention to Al. "Why didn't the residents of Fresno band together, arm themselves, and claim the land of their neighbors as their own?" he asked. When no reply was forthcoming, he continued, "Why accept living in a dismal, polluted, and unimportant dump?"

"Ah." Al slowly crossed his arms. "It's certainly a novel concept."

"Novel?" HCL scoffed. "It is hominid behavior that can be traced back to prehistoric times."

"Sure," Al conceded. "Way, way back then."

HCL tried to process this. "But not in twenty-first-century Fresno?" he probed.

"I'm afraid not."

"Despite the horrifying conditions of life there?" HCL pressed.

Al couldn't conjure up a better explanation. "It just wasn't done."

"Wasn't done?" HCL was having a hard time with the concept.

"You wouldn't get invited to any parties," Al said.

The mention of parties drew HCL's intense interest. "I see," HCL said slowly. "I rarely get invited to parties as it stands."

"All the more reason not to arm yourself, then," Al pointed out.

HCL came to some decision. "Indeed."

"Sorry I can't be of more use."

"That's quite all right," HCL told him happily. "In fact, I think I understand the nature of your era's political problems with more clarity than ever."

"You're welcome, I guess," Al said, feeling a bit out of his depth.

Al had to accept that this still wasn't going well. Before he could fully consider the implications of trying to talk to his wristband again, he was saved from further embarrassment by Joan's arrival. She was in such a hurry that she clipped the portal with her head as she ducked through before it had fully dilated.

"We've got a serious problem," she said, rubbing her head.

9

TIME, TO GO

JOAN STOOD flushed and out of breath. Lunch rested uneasily within her. Taking inventory, she noted that she was not nauseated or sick. The tremor in her gut, she realized, was an emotion that had become quite unfamiliar: unspeakable terror.

Impala squinted at Al as she continued the process of memorizing his vulnerable spots. "Don't tell me he killed Hitler."

"No!" Joan said. "No. Nothing like that. He passed the screening already."

"That's good." Impala sighed with relief.

"What is it with you people and Hitler?" Al ventured to ask.

Impala and Joan shared a knowing look, and Impala chuckled.

"We're protectors of the timeline, not assassins," Joan said.

"Can you imagine the mess we'd have to clean up if someone actually managed to off the bastard?" Impala shook her head.

"The DPA would never allow such an eventuality," HCL chimed in.

Joan grunted. "That's just it—I can't reach the DPA."

"Oh." Impala wiped her greasy hands on her habit as she stood. "Shit." Somehow the fabric didn't seem strong enough to contain her, as if the sharp edges of her joints threatened to tear through the uniform.

"We need to accelerate our mission timeline and begin our temporal excursion as soon as possible," Joan continued.

"Sounds like it," Impala grunted.

"What's going on?" Al asked.

"The DPA is the canary in the coal mine," Joan explained. "If we can't reach them, that means we're dealing with a major breach of space-time continuity, the kind of temporal malfeasance that could prevent Professor Filigree from ever inventing the time machine."

"And that's the bad part?" Al asked.

Joan tried to tunnel through to his currently limited understanding of space-time. "If Professor Filigree never founded The Institute, all of us here would cease to exist."

Al frowned. "That sounds painful."

Joan was encouraged. Maybe he was getting it. "We would be gone"—Joan snapped her fingers—"like that. There would be no time to feel pain."

Al accepted his annihilation by clicking his tongue. "What can we do about it?" he asked.

Joan addressed them all. "First, we're getting out of here before the ripple in space-time has a chance to catch up with us."

"Of course. That was my first guess," Al said.

HCL seemed discouraged. "We might be the only ones prepped for a temporal excursion with a negative entry point," he pointed out.

Joan put a hand on the cyborg's shoulder reassuringly. "The board gave us the go-ahead to expedite the temporal revision," she told them.

"So that's where you were," Impala groused. "We still haven't gone over the uniforms with you."

"We've wasted too much time already," Joan said defensively, eyeing HCL. "It was nearly impossible to constitute a quorum. Seems two of the board members never existed in the first place."

"That's troubling," HCL said.

"We're dealing with a catastrophic cascading paradox loop that could drastically alter the space-time continuum as we know it," Joan explained. "As we suspected, the incongruity seems to be originating in the early twenty-first century."

"That's my century!" Al noted with satisfaction. "Good old twenty-first."

"It's nothing to be proud of," Impala told him. "You didn't leave much of a planet for the rest of us."

"Tell that to the guy who invented the electric car," Al quipped.

"Actually, the electric car was invented in the early twentieth century," HCL informed him.

"Really? Then why did it take so long to . . ." Al let his thought trail off, jolted by the concerned look on Joan's face.

"The board has agreed to dispatch our team to the twenty-first century with all haste. I want everyone to perform a final equipment check and chronological survey."

"This is the team?" Al asked with a bit of dismay. "All of it?"

Joan smiled. "You're traveling with an elite force of timekeeping commandos trained to operate within hostile environments over the entire range of human existence. We travel in a small group to avoid detection. With our combined skillset, the three of us are capable of infiltrating and compromising the most secretive and paranoid organizations in human history. Still, nothing's as valuable as experience, so we bring along a local expert to help with the insertion."

"Who's our local expert?" Al asked.

Joan, Impala, and HCL turned to face him. Al thought they might be waiting for something.

"You are," Joan reminded him.

"Right." He tried to smile. "Of course. What's your role?"

"I'm in charge," Joan said plainly. "HCL is a temporal mechanic. Impala is our cultural ambassador."

"She's an ambassador?"

"People like me," Impala said with a shrug. She threw her toothpick over her shoulder. It landed back on the table with a clank. "It's not like I trashed the planet or anything."

"That's hardly my fault," Al said, though he'd begun to wonder himself.

"We can't waste time on a trip to the staging zone. We're going to remotely trigger the temporal excursion right here." Joan began to tap on her Almanac, which unlike Al's, seemed to have quite a few shiny buttons. They were brightly colored and in a neat little row. Suddenly Al felt quite envious of the buttons, buttons whose very existence he hadn't known of a few seconds earlier.

Al knew at that moment he would stop at nothing to get a row of shiny buttons.

"That's risky," HCL noted, looking over Joan's shoulder. "There's a significant chance of omniversal fallout. Should be interesting."

"What's risky?" Al asked. He tried to focus on the

answer, or at least appear to. It seemed so important. But even as Joan gestured emphatically and shouted at them, all he could see were the buttons on her wristband. Was that a toggle? Her wristband had a toggle!

" . . . And that risk will increase every moment that we wait," Joan finished.

"So, let's get it over with," Impala said.

"Prep for multiversal jump," Joan warned them.

"Get what over with?" Al said, having understood only that something terribly dangerous was about to happen. "Do you—"

"I don't have time," Joan spoke over Al's objections. "HCL, can you explain the technical details to our new recruit?"

HCL examined Aloysius for a moment. Then he turned back to Joan and shook his head. "No."

"Too busy?" Al asked hopefully. "Maybe when we have a spare minute?"

"You're not capable of understanding," HCL informed him coldly.

"I'm in tech myself, remember?" Al said, flicking away a piece of lint with practiced nonchalance.

HCL didn't seem impressed. "Don't take it personally. With your current intellectual capacity, you wouldn't grasp the underlying concepts. It would be as if I were merely stringing together vaguely technical words into a perfectly grammatical sentence that nonetheless conveyed no real information."

"You explained that in a way that was really easy to understand," Impala noted to HCL. "I think he'll get it."

"What? There's no need to treat me like I'm mentally deficient. I mean, it's not like I'm a Neanderthal."

"Whoa!" Impala snarled at him.

"Al!" Joan remonstrated.

"I find that sentiment to be highly offensive," HCL added.

Al looked around in confusion. "What did I say?"

"There are numerous Neanderthals working at The Institute," Joan said.

"Hang on. There are actual Neanderthals working at The Institute?"

"Of course," Joan said quietly. "Whenever a mission requires that we travel to their time period, we recruit a local expert to help with the insertion process." She looked at him pointedly. "Such as yourself."

"I'm quite sorry," Al said meekly. "It's a lot to get used to."

"Have you met Karl, in HR?" Impala asked him. "Recruited for one mission, now he runs half a department."

"There's a Neanderthal in Human Resources?"

"His *name* is Karl," Impala informed him.

Joan ended any further discussion. "Twenty seconds to multiversal jump," she announced with precision.

"Hang on," Al said desperately. "I . . ." he began, taking a long look at his three companions as he wondered what in the world he could say to end this grim delusion. "I'm not sure I'm packed for this," he blurted.

Impala snorted.

"Five seconds to multiversal jump," Joan intoned.

Then, as the universe collapsed and the very structure of space-time folded in on itself, Al had a horrifying realization: *None of them had brought a phone charger.*

10

DUST IN THE WORMHOLE

THE CREATION of a wormhole deep inside the gravity well of a planet is a stupendously risky endeavor. Unless you're actually *trying* to destroy the planet in question and eradicate all life upon it. In which case it's a pretty sure bet.

As a result of that risk, savvy time travelers don't actually go about creating any wormholes. Instead, they sift through the multiverse until they find a parallel universe identical to their own in every way, with the single exception being that the desired wormhole already exists within it. It was an impossible task, accomplished mostly by trial and error. Even Professor Edward Filigree, who'd invented the method, didn't really know how it was accomplished. But *it worked*. And that was the important thing.

If a time traveler somehow shifted to a parallel universe in which the wormhole's configuration was slightly off, then the planet and all life upon it would be eradicated. That is to say, it would have already been eradicated. Tragic, of course, but such an eventuality also ensured that there wasn't anyone around to complain about it. Professor Filigree's device left only very satisfied time travelers . . . and an infinite number of individuals whose planets had summarily ceased to exist. Those deceased copies didn't trouble him overly much, mostly because they couldn't get to a multiversal communicator and give him an earful. All that was left of them was dust in the wormhole.

Had anyone bothered to explain this to Aloysius before his first time jump—an infinite series of Earths would be created, and all but one immediately destroyed—he might have had second thoughts. He may even have had third thoughts and tied his personal record.

Joan had locked each of their Almanacs to her command unit, enabling her to override their space-time regulators and engage the portable time-travel units in unison. So, it could be argued that it was Joan who ultimately bore responsibility for the creation and destruction of so many parallel universes. She wasn't losing any sleep over it.

As Joan triggered the insertion procedure, a great ripple in actuality emerged from the depthless fathoms of possibility. The spring tide rose, snapping their anchor to causality and lifting Al and his compatriots out of the time stream. A current of change swept over prevailing reality. For no time at all they were adrift in impossibility, until the great wave of inevitability propelled them onward. Then, the waters of time receded just as precipitously as they had risen, depositing them roughly amid the swift flow of years.

A month tumbled past. Then the roiling torrent spun weeks on end. Aloysius tried to relax himself; he began to float, drifting between day and night. Looking down, Al realized he was just over an hour. It was an unpleasant hour, long and wasted, and he dreaded its approach. But before he knew it, a minute flew by, then another and another. He counted the minutes as they passed until they were too numerous to tell one from the next. Eventually Al heard the tick and tock of the seconds following him, and at the very last he remembered to steal a final moment when it flashed before him.

Suddenly, and without warning or reason, there was a great deal of screaming.

In this particular instance, Al was the only one screaming. It must be grudgingly admitted, he was quite good at it. His high-pitched warble carried for a great distance and seemed to pierce the eardrums with its volume and ferocity. Actually, it was a great deal like a klaxon, a sound that Al had become intimately familiar with only recently. But unlike a mechanical klaxon, designed specifically to cut through any lesser noise and demand the attention of all who could hear it, a human klaxon serves very little purpose. Especially when the human klaxon in question is just beginning his first clandestine incursion into the time-line, supposedly intent on leaving as small a footprint as possible on the temporal landscape.

Joan was rather used to the screams of the helpless and the victimized, having spent her formative years on and off the battlefields of the Hundred Years' War. Still, she was taken aback by the power of Aloysius' scream. First, she wasted precious time checking whether there was a band of marauding knights charging toward them. Then she squandered even more moments reminding herself that she no longer lived in fifteenth-century Normandy. Old habits die hard, especially those that are meant to preserve one's life in the face of a charging band of brutes.

Acutely aware of their need for secrecy, HCL began to synthesize a sedative that would render Aloysius unable to scream—or stand upright, for that matter. Although HCL's logical processor was a biomechanical computer so advanced that it made the human brain seem comparable to a walnut, he found the problem of the sedative took rather longer than he'd hoped. There were just so many variables. How much did Al weigh? Did he have any known allergies? Was he afraid of horses? What about camels? Did he have any known phobias whatsoever concerning domesticated quadrupeds of any sort?

And even for a cybernetic life form like HCL, the scream was very distracting.

Impala thought nothing at all, and so she was the first to react. Without compunction, she slapped Aloysius in the face and sent him falling to the pavement.

HCL, although aware that Impala had solved the immediate problem with remarkable dispatch, continued his calculations. Somehow, he had gotten the idea that keeping a dose of sedative around for Aloysius might come in handy sooner rather than later.

Before Joan resolved upon a course of action, she found herself holding Impala back. Joan was a bit surprised at her own instincts.

"What?" Impala asked her with a confused snarl.

Joan shook her head dumbly.

"What the hell was that about?" Al asked from the ground.

"We can't draw attention to ourselves," Joan explained.

"I wasn't," Al said defensively. He looked around, taking in the surroundings.

The first thing he noticed was that he was dressed as a pizza delivery driver, in shorts, a vest, and a matching cap. The Almanac around his wrist was disguised as a nifty smartwatch. Beside him stood an imposing nun, a bored firefighter, and a ticked-off flight attendant.

"You were screaming," Impala told him. She shrugged Joan off.

"I don't think I was screaming," Al said with a slightly patronizing tone.

"You were undoubtedly screaming," HCL said as he helped Al from the asphalt.

Al began to brush off his shirt. "I'm fairly certain I wasn't screaming."

HCL cocked his head. "I can replay my auditory records if you'd like."

Al froze self-consciously. "You're recording this?" he asked with suspicion.

"Of course."

"Isn't that a bit intrusive?" Al looked over his shoulders. No one else seemed to care.

"Intrusive?" HCL prompted incredulously.

"It's an invasion of my privacy," Al huffed.

"Ah, I see. Well then, is your short-term memory an invasion of my privacy?"

"I guess not," Al admitted.

"Then I fail to see why my own memory storage should be an issue."

"Good point," Al said, scowling. He couldn't help but resent the great unfairness of existence, despite having risen from the dead only a few hours prior.

"Al," Joan said in a gentle tone. He didn't respond. "Al!" She spun him around until they faced one another. "We need you to verify our temporal coordinates."

"I don't know our temporal coordinates!"

Joan sighed. "Are we in the twenty-first century, or not?"

Al brushed the wormhole dust off his pants and looked around.

11

BEST LITTLE CITY

THE FOUR TIMEKEEPERS stood on the sidewalk of a broad, sunny street that reeked of ozone and diesel. Beneath them the asphalt baked; above them a star shone only ninety-three million miles away.

Aloysius took a deep breath of contaminants and twirled around to bask in the twenty-first-century-ness of the whole thing. A semitruck blew by, horn blasting, spraying a cloud of gravel and dust over his pizza delivery driver outfit. "I never thought I'd see it again," he said contentedly.

"So, this is twenty-first-century Fresno?" Joan asked above the well-starched collar of her flight attendant's uniform.

"Yes," Al said. "There's no doubt about it."

"What's wrong with the air?" Impala asked warily. It was not without knowledge of the irony that a woman who'd been born and raised in a post-apocalyptic waste-land was asking about Fresno's air quality. "It smells like burning garbage," she added with a sniff, adjusting her wimple.

Al nodded. "Welcome to Fresno."

"How can you tell it's Fresno?" Joan asked. Before Al could answer, she turned to Impala, demanding, "Why am I dressed like this? I look ridiculous."

"You're wearing the uniform of a twenty-first-century flight attendant," explained Impala.

"Is that some kind of sex worker?" Joan asked, tugging at her skirt.

"In this era, a flight attendant brings people carbonated beverages on an airplane," HCL told her.

Joan adjusted her shoes with distaste. "Why would someone who serves drinks on a moving vehicle be wearing four-inch heels?"

"Hey, there's an old document-shredding business!" Al pointed at the back of a strip mall across the street.

"What an odd use for a building," the cyborg said, trying to get his helmet to sit at an appropriately jaunty angle.

"And there's a coffee shop!" Al shouted.

"There's two of them," Impala noted.

"Yes, but don't go to that one," Al put in quickly. "That one's terrible."

"They appear nearly identical," HCL added.

Al sighed. "It's just as I remembered it."

"How long has it been?" Impala asked him.

"From my perspective, it's been, oh . . . let's see . . . about half a day. But from the perspective of the left-behinds stuck here in the twenty-first century, it's been almost two years."

"That doesn't seem very long," Impala said.

"Two years! Can you believe it? My first trip into the future." Al began to chuckle. "The future!" He twirled around again with his arms outstretched and his fingers splayed.

Impala drew close to Joan and muttered, "I thought you said he passed the screening."

"He did." Joan watched with concern as Al's chuckles turned to cackles. "He has. I think this is just the way he acts," Joan said. Then she added, "You know, normally."

"Normally?" Impala asked.

"On a regular basis," Joan clarified.

"The future is now!" Al cried. He removed his heavily branded hat and threw it into the air, barely failing to catch it on the way down.

Impala stretched her impressive arms over her head and flexed her muscles. "Should I hit him again?"

"I think he'll calm down in a moment," Joan said.

HCL approached them. "This behavior is unlike any template in my database," he said. "Should we be concerned?"

"He'll calm down," Joan repeated. "Just give him a minute or two."

Al ran toward the street corner. "Look at this!" he shouted back to them. "They still have traffic lights. I remember these. Wait for it. It should turn green in a few seconds. Just watch." He was bouncing up and down. "There it goes," he said with a final jump. "Good old green. It's all starting to come back to me."

"He doesn't seem to be calming down," Impala said.

Al ran back the other direction. "See that? Fast food. I wonder if the fries are still salty. Come on!" Al began dragging on Joan's arm.

"We don't have time for this," Joan said.

"You can't visit early twenty-first-century America without trying the French fries. That'd be like going to France and not trying the baguette."

"I've never had a baguette," Joan pointed out.

Al waved it away. "Locals always skip the tourist stuff," he said.

"What's a France?" asked Impala.

Al chuckled. "Spoken like a true Cleveland-er. Cleveland-ite?" Al paused, then looked to Impala. "Help me out here."

"I'm not your therapist," Impala growled.

"I don't need a therapist," he snapped back.

"I am familiar with multiple forms of ancient hominid psychological treatment," HCL interjected.

"I'm not an ancient hominid!" Al said. He looked from Joan to Impala, finding no support in either quarter.

HCL considered him closely. "That depends on your perspective."

Al let go of Joan and rounded on the impertinent cyborg. "From my perspective, you're a talking microwave."

HCL smiled blandly. "Do you think this unprovoked hostility reflects a deep-seated sense of inferiority?"

Al shook his head. "You're not going to get me talking about my childhood."

"Interesting. Is there something about your childhood that makes you feel inferior?" HCL pressed.

"That's . . ." Al looked around in confusion, then took a moment to collect himself. "You're smart for a microwave."

"I'm 'smart'?" HCL asked, bristling. "All I've ever wanted was the approval of a squishy bag of mostly water."

"Who's squishy!" Al demanded.

"All right, everyone," Joan said, stepping between them. "Let's synchronize our Almanacs' chronometers."

"They don't just synchronize themselves?" Al asked her.

"Don't be ridiculous," she scoffed.

Impala looked around warily, sniffing the air. "What is that?" she said suspiciously.

"What?" Al asked.

"That smell," she nearly whimpered.

"It's pizza," Al said gleefully. "Forget the fries. We'll get a pizza!"

"No time for that. We have a schedule to keep, and very little time to prepare for the temporal alteration," Joan informed him. "Besides, we've all had pizza before."

"Oh, and have we all drunk water before? Have we all breathed oxygen?" Al snorted. "Doing it before has no bearing."

"I'd like a pizza," Impala said.

"See? Everyone wants a pizza." Al grinned with childish joy.

"I do not require sustenance at this time," HCL said.

"That's why you don't get a vote," Al told him.

"No one gets a vote," Joan said. "I'm in charge of this mission."

"And you're doing a bang-up job," Al assured her. "But you know what would push your approval rating through the roof?"

Joan grunted. "Pizza?"

"Wow, you're a natural leader," Al exclaimed.

"She's famous," Impala pointed out.

"And deservedly so," Al said magnanimously. "I mean, she was just about to suggest we go out for pizza. It would be a great way for the three of you to get acclimated to the twenty-first century—and quite the team-building exercise."

"Every temporal excursion has a strict timeline to

follow," Joan explained. "If we're even one minute late, we'll miss the alteration point—our only chance to safeguard the timeline."

"We've got time for pizza," Al insisted.

"The schedule doesn't allow for—"

"Let's ask the temporal mechanic," suggested Al.

"We are sufficiently cushioned from the wave of temporal instability," HCL told them. "It would not alter the risk of a causality cascade."

"There you go," Al said. "That was my next point."

"Fine," Joan said. "We need to eat, anyway."

"Most of us do," Impala said.

"I require sustenance," HCL added, "although my internal reactor is extremely efficient."

"Uranium doesn't count as sustenance," Impala told him.

"I also require various organic molecules for use in my matter synthesis module."

"See? He's hungry," Al said.

"I'm not hungry," HCL put in.

"He's so hungry he's getting delirious," Al said with great satisfaction.

Al led them to the closest pizza place—mercifully not the same chain that was printed all over his uniform. Before long they were drawing stares. Joan in particular grew increasingly aware that they were standing out in some way, attracting attention to themselves, but she couldn't put her finger on why.

"We need to find shelter, and get HCL access to the local databank," she told the group. "We're too exposed."

"We can get the pizzas to-go. Then we'll get a motel room with continental breakfast and free Wi-Fi. That should be easy," Al said. "But I'm not compromising on the continental breakfast."

"Isn't access to the local data sphere more important?" Joan asked him.

"Don't underestimate continental breakfast," Al said gravely.

"They don't look like monsters," Impala said as she examined the passersby.

"Monsters?"

"Open your eyes, before-timer!" Impala glared. "These are the people who doomed us."

"I don't think—"

"Your people filled the rivers and oceans with plastic," Impala continued with scorn. "They spread their garbage across the earth. This so-called civilization poisoned the air with abandon and hunted species to extinction as a pastime. They ate babies and enslaved the elderly! Your people are monsters."

"Quiet," Joan hissed at her.

A woman jogged by, turning her head to stare at them as she passed. She nearly hit a telephone pole.

"I don't think anyone's eating babies or enslaving elderly people," Al objected. "Are you thinking of that movie with the guy from—what was it? Uhm . . . I can never . . . damn. It's gone. What were you saying?"

"Your people destroyed the planet," Impala provided.

"Right." Al nodded. "Only it wasn't all of us, was it? Mostly it was the people with those big SUVs, lumbering around."

"SUVs?" Impala asked in puzzlement.

"Big ones. Burnt a lot of gas."

"The people were larger?" Impala said.

"The SUVs were bigger. We might have been able to stop it in time, if it hadn't been for those idiots in the—"

"They're all looking at us," Joan interrupted. "We need to determine why we're standing out."

"It's the outfits," Al told her.

"No. That's not it," Joan said, straightening her shirt self-consciously. "It's not the outfits."

"I'm telling you, it's the outfits." Al pulled his pizza delivery guy shorts down an inch or two.

Impala chafed beneath her wimple. Her feet kept catching at the bottom of her habit as she paced. "I look fucking ridiculous."

"You look like a nun," Al reminded her.

"No one else around is dressed like a nun," she finally noted.

"Of course not."

"This was an Almanac-approved choice," Impala said. "Why aren't there more nuns? Where are all the other nuns?"

As Al was to learn, the Almanac was a good general guide, but it wasn't foolproof. He pulled up the entry on personal attire, and the mellifluous voice began speaking in his mind.

"When considering wardrobe choices in the early twenty-first century, the wise time traveler would be well advised to select from one of many stock characters, rather than attempting to devise their own combination of clothing and accessories. Some useful archetypes include the Catholic nun, the firefighter, the pizza delivery driver, and the flight attendant. These archetypes will deter all but the most persistent individuals from attempting to converse with the time traveler, and any idiosyncrasies in one's behavior may be attributed to the oddness of the archetype, rather than an anachronism on the part of the time traveler.

"It is never wise for the timekeeper to adopt the uniform of a barista, police officer, or lifeguard. In each of these cases, the uniform will provoke an unpredictable and demanding set of responses from residents of the time period. Even with the aid

of the Almanac's translation algorithm and memetic regurgitator, the time traveler will be hard-pressed to convincingly respond to requests for a 'tall soy double mocha hold the whip,' to call in backup during an escalating domestic dispute, or to perform CPR on an unconscious tourist while wearing nothing but a skimpy bathing suit.

"Should the time traveler need to trespass into restricted areas or approach strangers, the simple addition of a bright lime-green vest and a clipboard will ensure their welcome in all but the most secure locations. Conversely, if they wish to avoid any prolonged contact, carrying a Bible and asking, 'Have you been saved?' is a tried-and-true strategy for avoiding conversation.

"See entries for 'Ritual Mutilation,' 'Adornment with Worthless Rocks,' and 'A Modern Heuristic Approach to Cravats'."

Despite Impala and HCL having followed the Almanac's instructions to the letter, what the Almanac hadn't spelled out, and what HCL and Impala had failed to infer, was that while four tires on a car driving by don't elicit much notice, a single tire rolling down the street will immediately catch the eye.

What is the lone tire missing? Context.

"A nun, a flight attendant, a firefighter, and a pizza delivery guy," Al listed. "It sounds like the beginning of a joke."

"I wanted to be a lifeguard," HCL confided. "I fail to understand the Almanac's logic. I am perfectly capable of performing all manner of first aid regardless of my state of undress."

"No, the Almanac was right about the lifeguard thing," Al said. He couldn't help but picture a shirtless cyborg running down the beach in slow motion.

"But I would have liked a whistle. I am not capable of whistling," HCL admitted. "See?" He blew through pursed lips and managed to spray a fine mist of spittle into Joan's face.

"We can get you a whistle," Joan relented, drying herself.

"And a skimpy bathing suit?" HCL added.

"I don't think many firefighters walk around in skimpy bathing suits," Joan told him.

"You'd be surprised," Al said. "I've seen the calendars."

12

TRIAL BY ARMANI

IT WASN'T hard for Al to find a mediocre hotel in Fresno. It would have been harder to walk through town without happening upon one. HCL had convinced an ATM machine to cough up a huge stack of twenties, more than enough to keep the four of them knee-deep in pizza and safely housed in a mostly clean box of anonymity. Snug in their room at the La Loma Inn, HCL sat on one queen bed, Joan and Impala on the other. Al was sprawled on the floor. He would have been happy just to get a good night's sleep.

Joan, however, had other plans. Other plans are a bit like the neighbors' Wi-Fi—easy to ignore until they start interfering.

"We have sixteen hours," Joan told them, watching with revulsion as Impala ate the last slice of pepperoni.

"We can always extend the reservation," Al said from the floor.

"No." Joan glared at him. "I mean we have sixteen hours until the rogue alteration."

"With four of us, that's probably . . ." Al tried to perform some simple algebra. "Twelve large pizzas?"

"Will you forget about the pizzas!" Joan could feel the headache coming.

"I'm the pizza delivery guy," he said. "It's my job."

"Your job is to make us look like we belong in the twenty-first century," she reminded him.

Al snorted. "Then we should be eating more pizza."

Joan shook her head. "We need to perform reconnaissance on the arena."

"Arena?" Impala asked, suddenly perking up.

"And we need to establish our positions before the doctors gather," Joan went on.

"Is it some type of gladiatorial event?" Impala continued, growing more interested.

"It's a medical convention," Joan told her. "Don't you ever read the briefings?"

"Actually, no. Pretty much never."

"Think a thousand podiatrists from across the country all converging on Fresno for three days," Al said.

"And I'd like to try a dry run, if possible," Joan added.

"That's . . ." Al stopped. "All that sounds like we could take care of it in a couple hours at the most."

Joan waved him away dismissively. "And we should secure our equipment."

"Equipment?" Al made incredulous noises. "HCL has rocket hands!"

"I'm familiar with his—" Joan began.

"Show her!" Al urged the cyborg. "Start the countdown, or whatever."

"There's no need," Joan tried.

"I do not wish to risk the safety of our team unnecessarily," HCL added.

"See? Too dangerous to even show us." Al had decided to act as if he'd won the argument. It was a tactic that he loudly insisted had always worked for him.

"The chance of my armament damaging your being is small, but not insignificant," HCL admitted.

"Armament!" Al chuckled. "I get it. Rocket hands."

"No such joke was intended. But I value your contribution nonetheless."

Al smiled. "It's nice to be valued."

"Then you'll be pleased to learn that you may be even more valuable later as bait."

"Bait?" Al squeaked.

"Or as a diversion."

"A diversion?" Al repeated.

"Or perhaps as a voice recording device."

"A voice . . ." Al came to understand much the same

way a crash test dummy comes to a stop. "Oh. You're making fun of me."

"Indeed."

Al scratched the back of his head. "Then can I borrow one of your rocket hands?"

"I do not wish to risk damage to my appendage," said HCL indignantly.

Al tried to look offended. "But you want me to risk this whole squishy bag of water that keeps me inside it!"

"That is incorrect," HCL told him solicitously. "You're not *inside* the bag; you *are* the bag."

"Either way it's a rather important bag, and it's full of a very important liquid," said the indignant bag. "It has a terrible tendency to leak after just the slightest bit of shooting or swordplay or lasers or whatever," the bag added, sloshing around.

"Gentlemen? We're here for a reason," Joan said. "The clock is ticking every moment that you squabble."

"You see? Stop holding out on me. I need the rocket hand for the sake of the timeline. Isn't that what really matters? We're saving the people of Fresno!" Al nearly shouted.

Silence filled the small hotel room like candy in a piñata.

"We're making sure the bomb explodes, killing one hundred and fourteen," Joan said, her hand again on her forehead. It was hard not to see the writing on the wall when someone kept spelling it out.

"Are you sure we . . .?" Aloysius asked no one in particular. "I could have sworn we were doing the other."

Only Joan met his eye. "We're protecting the timeline," she said steadily. "It's the only way we can be sure that history won't be changed for the worse—even accidentally. Saving a pregnant woman today could result in the birth of a psychopath tomorrow."

"Even a minor deviation can have vast unintended consequences," HCL explained.

"It's why nobody's killed Hitler," Impala said, adding, "although most of us have thought about it."

"Excuse me," Al said as he stood. "I need to use the little boys' room."

Ensconced in the bathroom with the door locked behind him, Al began to run the water in the sink. When it was loud enough, he let himself cry.

Why couldn't he get the damn Almanac off his arm? It looked like a smartwatch now. He pulled and pulled, but it wouldn't budge. How was he going to get away from these lunatics?

As he collected himself, Al heard someone shuffling by the door.

"Knock-knock." The voice was muffled.

Al groaned, realizing he had no choice but to suffer

through more cyborg humor in a misplaced attempt to cheer him up. "Who's there?"

"It is I, HCL."

"HCL who?" he asked, reluctantly playing along.

"I was unaware that you were familiar with multiple HCL units. My personal designation is HCL-45R-37K."

Had any crickets managed to survive on the desolate streets of Fresno, their voices might have been heard.

"That wasn't funny," Al said as he opened the door.

"Indeed." HCL stood in the doorway.

"We'll work on it," Al assured him. "You'll be getting laughs in no time."

HCL tilted his head. "I was not attempting to engage in a humorous exchange at this juncture."

"But you said, 'Knock-knock'."

"Yes, I was requesting permission to enter the bathroom."

"See?" Al said. "This is why we need a signal!"

"According to the Almanac, 'Knock-knock' is a widely accepted signal used to express a desire to enter personal space."

"Sure," Al said. "But it's also a joke."

"I fail to see what's humorous about it."

"I'm not going to be the one defending knock-knock jokes," Al said with exasperation. "I don't find them funny myself."

HCL cocked his head. "Yet you attempted to engage me in one."

"It was just a misunderstanding," Al said, embarrassed for no good reason.

"I see," HCL said. "May I enter?"

"Sure." Al closed the toilet lid and took a seat. "Come in."

"I have no desire to enter," HCL stated. "It was a trivial untruth intended to elicit laughter."

"Wow," Al said, releasing a tremendous breath. "All that? It really didn't work."

"Regardless, I need your assistance with this groin-adjacent device I appropriated from the clerk."

Al blinked. "Excuse me?"

HCL held out a notebook computer. "A . . . laptop?" he continued.

"Open it up."

"I will fabricate the appropriate tools," HCL suggested, engaging his internal matter synthesis module with an audible whir.

"No, you . . ." With a sigh, Al led him out of the bathroom and to one of the two queen beds. There, he got HCL started with the *notebook* computer. It was a new experience for the cyborg, fascinating and delightful. For Al, observing over the cyborg's shoulder, it was pure torture. It turns out that not all cybernetic beings instinctively know how to use a keyboard and touchpad.

As he watched the cyborg slowly hunt and peck his way through a simple search, Al grew impatient. "Can't you just plug directly into the computer? Wouldn't that be faster?"

"Physically interface with the computer?" HCL shuddered.

"Yeah," Al said, oblivious to his discomfort. "Just pop in a USB and have at it."

HCL turned to face him. "Aloysius, if you were to find yourself in fifteenth-century France, would you seek to copulate with every harlot on the streets of Paris?"

"Of course not," Al sputtered, wondering if he should clear his browser history.

"And I will not expose myself to a foreign network from the twenty-first century." HCL went back to typing.

Al nodded. "Viruses."

"Among other things," said HCL. "There it is! Why are there fourteen letters on the left side, and only twelve on the right?"

"I'm not sure," Al admitted.

"It is a most irregular layout," HCL went on.

"Just seven more letters to go."

"Am I the only one trying to stick to the schedule?" Joan asked. "We only get one chance at this."

"Doesn't the schedule include time for acclimating to the twenty-first century?" Al pointed out. "This is important."

"How can we acclimate to the twenty-first century while we're stuck in a little room staring at a computer?" Joan objected.

"Actually," Al told her, "that would be close to ideal."

HCL let out a cry of delight. "I found the letter," he said with satisfaction. "I see you now, you little *u*. He's a mischievous one. I've got this under control." HCL smiled with satisfaction. "Six more to go."

"And you say you've never learned to type?" Al muttered.

"Not on a keyboard. No." HCL hovered his index finger over one key and the next as he searched. "Ah, there it is. I had found the *m* earlier, but it seems to have moved."

"The keys don't move," Al said.

HCL paused. "Are you certain of that?"

"Yes. Fairly certain." Al watched HCL flounder with rapidly growing impatience. "I can type that last part for you, if you'd like."

"No. Interfacing with anachronistic technology is part of my role as temporal mechanic."

"Right, of course it is," Al said. "But it might be faster if you just dictated to me, and I . . ." He saw HCL shaking his head. "Maybe you'll get used to it."

"I hope I do not have enough time to acclimate to this device," said HCL with evident distaste.

"Fine," Al agreed with a humph. "Leave me to be the only useful one around here."

"I have seen little evidence of productivity on your part," HCL told him.

"I resent that. I resented it when my mother said it. I resented when my guidance counselor said it. And now, I resent it when you say it."

"Useless," Joan added from the other bed. "You're a useless pizza delivery boy."

Al frowned. "Pizza delivery man," he said.

"Pizza delivery person," Impala suggested.

"Who stopped Impala from eating that dog?" Al went on. "Who introduced HCL to the ice machine?"

"Humph. She wasn't very talkative," HCL muttered.

"And . . ." Al paused, building up the drama a bit before he brought the full force of his argument to bear, "Who got all the pizza?"

"He did get a lot of pizza," Impala pointed out, her mouth full.

"See?" Al asked Joan.

"I still don't understand why I couldn't just eat the dog," Impala said under her breath.

"But did she eat it?" Al asked with a flourish. "No!" he shouted triumphantly.

"You've made your point," Joan said with a reluctant grin.

The Everyday Timekeeper's Almanac had this to say on the topic of canines in the early twenty-first century:

"Although a visitor to the twenty-first century will only rarely encounter horses, cattle, or other working animals, they are almost certain to encounter a great number of dogs out and about. Indeed, the dogs are so numerous and vital an accessory to the twenty-first-century resident that there is signage to point out the few places a dog may not accompany their person.

"It is absolutely vital that time travelers not stare at or remark upon any persons cleaning up the feces of dogs. It is best to ignore the matter entirely. Likewise, if anyone is seen walking with a dog leash in one hand and a small plastic bag in the other, under no circumstances should a timekeeper accept delivery of the bag! Despite the fixation on picking up their canine companion's feces, twenty-first-century residents allow their dogs to urinate anywhere and everywhere without mention. Another person's bike, a communal bench, the side of a building—all are fair game for the dog to 'mark' as his or her territory. It is incumbent upon the time traveler to stay out of the splash zone.

"Timekeepers must keep in mind that maintaining friendly relations with the canine companions of the twenty-first century is essential."

It was very good advice, and exceedingly difficult for someone born in twenty-third-century Cleveland to follow. The only canines Impala had ever met had been the feral packs that hunted her through the ruins of Ohio, the formerly domesticated dogs that had quite quickly become wolves once again.

"I've completed a search of the local data sphere," HCL told them. "I was unable to locate anything that might lead us to the rogue time travelers."

"Nothing at all suspicious?" Impala asked.

"That is correct."

"No unauthorized revisions?" Joan prompted.

"None that I can detect"—HCL gestured at the laptop —"at least given the primitive state of my tools."

"No UFO sightings? Flying saucers? That sort of thing?" Joan continued.

"None that have been reported."

"Flying saucers?" asked Al. He hated feeling left out. "I don't get it."

"The flying saucer is a common design for a cheaply manufactured time machine," HCL told him.

"So, all the reports of UFOs are really . . ." Al couldn't quite make it to the end of his thought.

"Amateur historians and budding scholars," HCL explained, "who have traveled back in time to conduct research."

"It's a scourge of doctoral candidates," Joan said. "So

desperate to be published they're willing to risk the entire course of human history." She threw her hands up. "I know, right? Their advisors should really address the issue while they're still undergrads, but nobody's asking me."

"Grad students?" Al asked. "Grad students are abducting people?"

"It's a lot easier than getting tenure the old-fashioned way."

"Lighten up," Impala told her. "You know how kids can be," she said, and waved away any lingering concern.

"Hominid adolescents have a well-known predilection for mischief," HCL added.

"We used to egg Mr. McGovey's house," Al admitted. It was the most innocent anecdote he could recall. Still Joan shook her head at him. "What?" Al asked her. "He gave out raisins on Halloween."

"What's so offensive about dried fruit?" HCL asked.

"I would have killed a man for a piece of dried fruit," Impala said.

"You would have felt pretty bad about it once you'd tried the raisins."

"I tricked my brother into eating a live scorpion once," Impala said, smiling at the memory.

"You what?"

"It was funny," Impala said.

"That doesn't sound funny."

"You had to be there."

"Let's get back on topic," Joan called out.

"Come on, Joan," Al urged, "you must have gotten into trouble as a kid."

"No, not really," she said.

"Nothing?"

"Well . . . my neighbor," Joan said with a sigh.

"What?" Al pressed. "What about your neighbor?"

"When I was a girl, I accused my neighbor of cursing my sheep."

"Cursing your sheep?" Impala asked. "That's it?"

Joan shuffled her feet. "And speaking in tongues."

"You started a witch hunt?" Al said, finally understanding.

Joan's cheeks reddened. "She was acting very suspicious."

"She wasn't burned at the stake or anything, was she?" Al asked.

"No," Joan said indignantly. She added, "She wasn't really a witch."

"That's a relief," Al said. "How did you figure it out?"

"They threw her in the river, and luckily she drowned." Halfway through this statement Joan had begun to lose her usual confidence.

"She drowned?" Al said, shocked.

"Well, witches float."

"The logic of ancient legal systems continues to escape me," HCL said.

"Case closed, I guess," Al said. "That's ironclad reasoning."

"A witch would have floated," Joan repeated.

Impala snorted. "Throwing someone into a river is a terrible way to tell if they're a witch."

"Thank you," Al said. "It's horrible."

"What you want to do is bake a cake using their urine, and feed it to a dog."

"Bake what?" Al asked, dismayed to think of any baked goods suffering such indignity. "I don't think that's going to work either."

"And if the dog eats it," Joan said, "the person must be a witch." She nodded thoughtfully.

"Not just that," Impala added. "You've got to watch the dog for a while and see if it starts behaving strangely."

"It's the accusers who are behaving strangely," Al put in. "They're the ones feeding urine cakes to perfectly friendly canines."

"HCL, have there been any surges of ionized anti-matter since our arrival?" Joan asked, eager to change the subject.

"None that I've detected."

"What about Bigfoot sightings?" Impala added.

"Bigfoot? Are they more PhD candidates?" Al asked. He had shown more curiosity in the last hour than he had in five years of high school.

"No," Joan explained. "Their physical appearance is

the natural result of hominids adapting over time to the eternal cold of a nuclear winter. They sometimes travel to the distant past for a nice vacation in the sun."

"But they're always walking around naked," Al pointed out.

Joan shrugged. "It's very hot for them in this era; they're used to the Ice Age."

"And they're only spotted in the remote forest!" he added.

Impala snorted. "You think they'd travel to the twenty-first century to talk to the people? You guys aren't exactly popular with the whole 'we didn't destroy the planet' crowd."

"There have been no recent Bigfoot sightings," HCL told them. "Although I am seeing reports that a half-man half-bat was born to a lovely woman in Skokie." He faced the laptop toward the others so they could see the social media post for themselves. "And these two here"—HCL pointed to an attractive couple pictured on the screen—"It would seem they're getting divorced, and many people are in a terrible state of suffering over it."

Al let out a long sigh. "Next you're going to tell me that Santa Claus is a time traveler."

"Al, you know that Santa isn't real, right?" Impala asked him quietly.

"I don't know what to believe anymore," Al said.

"What you are experiencing is called delirium temporal," HCL told him.

"Sounds more like chronic vertigo," Impala suggested.

HCL began, "Although they frequently have comorbidity, chronic vertigo usually presents—"

"I don't care what it's called." Al moaned. "How do I get rid of it?"

"It will lessen with time," Joan assured him. "For now, I suggest you rely on the team's judgment when you're experiencing an attack."

"Wonderful," Al said. "I should trust Impala, the woman who almost ate a dog."

"Delirium temporal is a common affliction among ancient hominids during their first few temporal excursions," HCL said. "There's very little we can do to speed your recovery."

"Thanks a lot, Gort," Al snapped.

HCL stiffened. "That is an incorrect appellation. Please refer to me as HCL."

Al scoffed wordlessly, a sound very much like the vocalization of an exhausted walrus as it pulled itself out of the ocean and onto a particularly uncomfortable ice floe. "What's it matter to a microwave?" he added, by way of human speech.

"One is my name; the other is not. And Gort was much taller," HCL told him with remarkable patience. "And shiny."

"Trust what you can see, what you can smell," Impala said, completely ignoring HCL. Having worked with the cyborg for a few subjective years, Impala had a great deal of practice ignoring him, and was always eager to hone her skills.

"All I can smell is pizza," Al told her.

"Then pizza's real," Impala assured him.

Joan and HCL began to put their heads together. "Perhaps our presence has already interfered with the historical nexus to such an extent that the detection of the rogue time traveler is all but impossible," HCL said. "It may be wise to return to the staging zone."

"We're not giving up," Joan told him.

HCL went on, "We may have violated the Triple P just by—"

"If that were the case, we never would have gotten the go-ahead for the insertion," Joan objected. "That's exactly the sort of thing the Department of Paradox Avoidance is supposed to prevent."

"Not necessarily, particularly if there wasn't enough information in the historical record for the DPA to accurately identify the event."

"I thought the Department of Paradox Avoidance had ceased to exist?" Al pointed out.

The timekeepers turned to him with a gasp.

"Don't say that!" Joan shushed him.

"What?"

"We don't know that anything's 'ceased to exist'," Joan insisted. She elbowed him. "Right?"

But Al didn't not know. He *knew*. It was one of the only things Al did know, as a fact, and he was reluctant to relinquish his knowledge just because a historical religious figure was peer-pressuring him. "That's what the Almanac told me," he insisted.

"I'm not hearing this," Impala muttered.

"Listen, the DPA seems to disappear every other week," Joan told him. "The important thing is to give it a chance to come back."

"I'm not stopping it," Al protested.

Impala snarled. "If you keep talking about it, you certainly will be."

"I don't see how talking about it could hurt."

"That's because you don't know the first thing about temporal mechanics," Joan told him crossly.

"Witnessing an alteration in the timeline can initiate a recursive causality loop," HCL explained with more patience than a saint.

"What's a recursive causality loop?"

"A self-fulfilling prophecy," Impala said, "a violation of the Triple P."

"Triple P?"

"Predestination Paradox Protocols," HCL added. "It becomes much harder to reverse, especially when the alteration occurs before the incursion's zero point."

"You see? You probably just misheard the Almanac," Joan added, nodding.

"It was speaking directly in my head," Al pointed out.

"Then you didn't understand it," Joan quickly put in.

"I certainly didn't understand it," Al agreed readily.

"Good. That's good." Joan had relaxed again. At least as much as Joan ever relaxed: One of her shoulders was slightly less tense than it had been. "He didn't understand what he was hearing," she said to the others with satisfaction.

"Should I kill him, to preserve the timeline?" Impala asked her.

"No," Joan said quickly, "of course not."

"Why would you kill me?" Al asked with considerable concern and a bit of surprise. He thought they'd been getting along nicely.

"I don't know," Impala admitted. "This time-travel stuff can be confusing. I like to trust my instincts." She turned to the cyborg. "HCL? Any insight?"

"I don't see how that course of action would help to avoid a temporal paradox," he informed her.

"Yeah, but would it hurt?" Impala asked, just to be certain.

"It would be unlikely to affect it either way," HCL told her.

"Good enough." Impala cracked her knuckles.

"No one's killing anyone!" Joan shouted, stepping between them. "She's kidding, Al."

"I was being serious," Impala protested, adding, "It's for the sake of the timeline."

"She's kidding," Joan insisted.

Impala shrugged. "Suit yourself. You're the one always saying, 'for the good of human history,' and all that crap."

"Nobody's getting killed," Joan told them. After an awkward pause, she added, "Except for the people at the medical convention."

"Little Ms. Sunshine," Impala crooned.

"Let's get some sleep," Joan suggested. She looked at Al shrewdly. "I can't stress enough that we'll be on a very tight schedule from here on out."

13

A FANCY PASSING

LATE THE NEXT MORNING, La Loma Inn's assistant hotel manager suffered a disturbing and disagreeable hallucination. At least, in the aftermath of the incident, Assistant Hotel Manager Anne Dreffel convinced herself that it had been a brief hallucination. For all she knew, it could just as easily have been a momentary delusion, or maybe even a passing fancy.

Anne would go on to tell quite a few psychiatrists, psychologists, and even a chiropractor about the morning in question, all of whom thought the stories were either a benign form of psychosis or the root of a lot of tension near her C7 vertebra. To each of them, Anne would relate that although later she felt quite convinced that she'd been in a delusional state, at the time she could have sworn that an extremely rude nun and a scatterbrained pizza delivery boy in revealing shorts were haranguing her about a missed wake-up call.

The irate guests—who, Anne insisted, were possibly figments of her imagination—demanded that she reprimand whoever it was who'd forgotten to wake them, something not just unwarranted but downright impossible. She tried to explain to the guests that no actual people were involved when a wake-up call was ordered at La Loma Inn, but the nun in particular was entirely unreasonable about the situation. She did grow a bit more sympathetic once Anne got into explaining the computerized nature of the wake-up service, muttering something about "knowing the type" and gesturing dismissively at some absent tormentor.

Given their evident distress, Anne couldn't help but feel that she—and indeed the entire La Loma Inn family— had let down these guests in a most extraordinary manner. But she couldn't quite understand how, or why. To Anne's relief, a very serious flight attendant came to join them, and for a brief instant Anne felt sure this authority figure would have a salubrious effect. But her arrival didn't much improve the situation. The only difference in the flight attendant's demeanor was that she wasn't only yelling at Anne, but also at the other guests. Anne thought their near hysteria over the missed wake-up call was entirely unwarranted—especially considering the ubiquity of cell phones. Who wouldn't just set the alarm on their phone?

Strangely enough, on numerous occasions during their conversation, the nun seemed baffled by the use of her own cell phone, though she did pull it out and poke it every few minutes. Seeing her mindlessly poking at the cell phone reassured Anne, who was much taken with the practice herself. Still, she couldn't help but notice that the nun's poking seemed to be of the random variety. Who would poke their phone at random when there were apps to swipe and shiny icons to tap?

That settled things for Anne, and led her to a troubling conclusion: These guests were *eccentric*. Anne liked eccentrics generally, but once specifics got involved the whole thing became a nightmare. In this decidedly specific instance, Anne found herself suddenly desperate to redeem La Loma Inn in the eyes of this quarrelsome trio.

It may seem odd to those unfamiliar with twenty-first-century corporate culture, but the staff of La Loma Inn prided themselves on something. Given the modest nature of the establishment, most of them didn't really know what exactly it was that La Loma Inn was proud of, but that didn't stop the staff from declaring their pride loudly and often. Admittedly, it could feel a bit silly to produce much bluster under the circumstances, but the staff of La Loma Inn consoled themselves with the thought that this stubborn pride-taking was itself something to be proud of. The legitimacy of her pride having been satisfied in a curiously circular manner, Anne felt just as much nonspecific pride as the rest of them. At least she had until that morning.

Considering Anne's distinct feeling of shame, when the flight attendant mentioned their urgent need to hire a carriage, she leapt at the chance to prove herself. Demonstrating the ride-hailing app on her phone, Anne walked the curious group through the process. Then she went over it again with the newly arrived firefighter, who was insistent that he be the one holding the phone even though it was Anne filling in their particulars. It was interminable. For a group so worked up on their adherence to schedule, they wasted an awful lot of time arguing over the size of car they would need.

The pizza delivery boy, who Anne had only minutes earlier identified as the only source of sanity in the room, almost entirely neglected the ride-hailing app, bent as he was on devouring as much of the breakfast buffet as humanly possible in the short span of time allotted. Every once in a while, he would burble delightedly and express deep admiration for what he repeatedly and pointedly referred to as the "continental breakfast." When Anne tried to explain that the pastries and coffee were, in fact, merely a breakfast buffet, the pizza delivery boy jumped up and down and howled in frustration. Far from dissuading him, the knowledge spurred on ever-greater attempts to shove the entire buffet of muffins and stale coffee into his mouth.

By the time the flight attendant and the firefighter had finished arguing over the difference between a "luxury car" and a "select model," the pizza delivery boy was nearly in tears, still pawing at the breakfast buffet ineffectually but unable to stomach another bite. The flight attendant tried to pull him away, but the young man in short shorts was surprisingly strong for someone who seemed to be suffering from acute hypoglycemia. He pushed the flight attendant away, and she stumbled into the nun with a mutter of apology.

To the best of what Anne sincerely hoped was her flawed recollection, in response to the provocation the nun growled out a bitter rejoinder and began impugning the ancestry of the pizza delivery boy in graphic detail. He shouted back something about doubting the anthropogenic basis of climate change, which, judging from the nun's sudden and frightening rage, was a sore subject for the clergywoman—a very sore subject.

At that moment Anne discovered that before you'd seen a nun sprint across the lobby of a mediocre hotel and wrestle a pizza delivery person to the floor, you didn't really understand the phrase "wrath of God." The strange combination of piety and violence was terrifying, titillating, and ultimately just silly. In Anne's estimation, nothing could have made the scene more absurd—but Anne's estimation hadn't taken into account the flight attendant, who was, it must be said, extremely cantankerous even for someone working at a domestic airline.

The flight attendant entered the fray by yanking on the

nun's wimple. Immediately the nun's head snapped back, and with a snarl she spun to confront her attacker. The frocked pugilist threw a tremendous punch, but the flight attendant sidestepped with remarkable grace, especially impressive considering her extremely impractical shoes. Undeterred, the nun renewed her assault. A right hook, a jab, a knee to the groin—each of her attacks was blocked or dodged with ease. The nun's blows grew more desperate and wild, until she was throwing her whole body into each attack with abandon. Still the flight attendant diverted the attacks without even wrinkling her uniform. The nun's panting grew heavy, her limbs slow. Eventually the flight attendant took the opportunity to push the nun to the ground, where the sister collapsed and lay gasping like an exhausted preschooler after four hours in the ball pit.

Around then the firefighter exclaimed that his communication device was making a peculiar noise and shifting itself about as if it were a living thing. Having finally pulled himself from what little was left of the breakfast buffet, the pizza delivery boy had improved enough to sarcastically explain ringtones and vibrating alerts to the baffled emergency worker. Apparently, their ride was out front.

At this, the flight attendant turned from the nun—still recovering on the floor—and began to speak in a surprisingly inspiring manner. Despite not understanding even half of what the flight attendant was saying, for some reason Anne felt ready to face down a band of knights charging toward a battle. Prior to this, Anne had been unwilling to face down even a band of toddlers charging toward a ball pit, so this change was quite an improvement.

From what the flight attendant shouted as she shook her fist, Anne gathered that some kind of history class was going to be tremendously disappointed with the change in schedule, though what that schedule had entailed and why it was so important, she never quite understood. Anne offered to walk them to their car, but the flight attendant insisted they'd had more than enough of an impact on Anne's life already.

Anne didn't disagree.

14

KILLING TIME

"WHY DOES the car not rid itself of the meddlesome human and drive itself?" HCL wondered rather loudly.

"What's that?" the meddlesome human in question asked from up front.

The four timekeepers were squished into an electric car along with the driver—a large man in a small shirt who had embraced the gig economy wholeheartedly but antiperspirant only tepidly.

"Ignore him," Al told the driver. "He's still learning English." Then Al turned to the cyborg, and added with a whisper, "The car can't get rid of the human."

"More ludicrous twenty-first-century legal theory," HCL said with scorn. "I suppose they have to consult the local oracles first, kill a raven or something."

"No, it's . . ." Al shook his head. "The car can't even drive itself."

"Impossible," HCL pronounced. Then he turned for a closer look at Al, and asked, "Is this an attempt at humor?"

"It's true," Al assured him.

"There's very little in the way of barricades," Joan was saying from the front seat as she surveyed the ground. "One cavalry charge and—"

"The flight attendant's pulling my leg, ain't she, sister?" the driver asked Impala, squinting at her in the mirror.

"I am not your sister," Impala said, glaring at the driver like she was ready to punch him. Basically just her normal expression, really.

"That's what most people call a nun, sister," Joan reminded her from the passenger seat.

"Of course," Impala snarled. She turned back to the driver. "None of us are pulling or otherwise touching your leg."

"Then the corpulent man in front is . . . driving?" HCL asked, very loudly and with a great deal of skepticism.

"Yes," Al said, adding, "and he can hear you." Though HCL was in every other way vastly superior to a toaster, the toaster just edged him out when it came to discretion. Al was glad it was Joan sitting in the front. She would have passed as a completely normal twenty-first-century resident. If it weren't for the total lack of an airport.

"Advance no farther," Joan told the driver. "We'll approach on foot."

"Right over here, please." Al said. "That'll be fine," he

continued, his twenty-first-century instincts taking over. "Thanks."

"Hit my band up on YouTube," the driver suggested with a smile.

"I'll absolutely check out your band."

"Thanks. You can always find us at the old Chili's on the third Thursday of every other month."

As the four timekeepers climbed out of the car, the dull heat of a Fresno day hit them like a sledgehammer.

"Oh goddammit. Don't touch anything metal," Al warned them. "It gets hot."

"Hear that, bolt head?" Impala asked with a grin.

"My hearing is vastly superior to your own," HCL replied.

"My hearing is vastly superior to your own," Impala mimicked.

HCL pretended not to hear.

"It's larger than I expected," Joan said, examining the exterior of Byers Arena. "We'll have to move quickly if we're to get back on schedule."

No windows, Joan noted at once. In fact, there were few entrances at all in the wide concrete facade. Above the main doors was an enormous image of two mighty warriors leaping into battle. *There must be murder holes,* she told herself. Nearby a sally port was covered with a thick steel door. The land around the arena had been cleared, leaving no structures or trees, nothing to offer shelter. *A killing field.* Joan grunted with admiration and dismay.

"We'll find another way in," she told them.

"The side entrance?" Al suggested.

"Yes," Joan agreed, "the side entrance."

"There's a lot of space in Fresno," Al said as they hurried through a nearly empty parking lot. He couldn't wait to get back into the air-conditioning.

"Isn't space equally large from any position?" HCL asked.

"Stay alert," Joan said uneasily. She ducked behind a metal obstruction and peeked around the corner. She didn't see a single guard patrolling the crenellations, but that didn't mean some weren't waiting for them out of sight.

"Alert for what?" Al asked, strolling past the silver minivan obliviously.

"I think he's right," Impala admitted to Joan, eyeing the ancient temple with disgust. "You're looking kind of suspicious," she added, tugging on her wimple.

Reluctantly, Joan relinquished her cover and strode into the open. "We have one hour until the alteration point, if everything proceeds according to the timeline," she told them.

"What's the chance of that?" Al asked. Then he looked at the cyborg. "HCL?"

HCL had been momentarily distracted by a nifty red

sports car that was, for some reason, rudely ignoring him. "The chance of what?" he asked, turning back to the group.

"What are the odds our mission will all work out?" Al gestured to the world at large. "That 'everything proceeds according to the timeline'?"

"The odds? Impossible to know," HCL said in a disgruntled voice. "How could I calculate the probability of such an event? The variables would be astronomically complex."

"Spock always makes a guess," Al huffed. "What about a guess?"

HCL grimaced. "I am uncomfortable making premature conclusions given the lack of data."

"How about a guesstimate?" Al pressed.

"My assumptions would be unsupported," HCL pointed out. "It would not be—"

"A rough guesstimation, maybe?" Al suggested, quickly adding, "Just back-of-the-envelope kind of stuff."

"I'd be curious myself," Joan added reluctantly.

"Spill it," Impala snorted.

"Very well. With the proviso that my 'rough guesstimation' will be a wildly inaccurate and unscientific endeavor that's not to be relied upon."

"Got it." Al nodded. "What are our odds?"

"Considering we are dangerously off schedule as a result of the wake-up call fiasco, I calculate the odds stand at approximately three billion to one against the successful completion of our mission," HCL replied without further hesitation.

"Wow. I wasn't expecting that." Aloysius took a deep breath. "That's hard to hear."

"As I previously warned," HCL began, "the margin of error in such a calculation—"

"Dark," Al said, shaking his head. "That's bleak. I'm not sure I can go through with this."

"Maybe keep it to yourself next time, sunshine," Impala muttered to the cyborg.

Even in his despondent state, Al noted a man headed into the arena in the distance, wearing something uncannily like tights and a cape. No one else had seen anything unusual. Al shuddered to think of the indignities a pharmaceutical rep would suffer in order to hobnob at a medical convention.

"Move out," Joan said. "And stay close." She headed to the side entrance, pulling Al close to her side.

The drive had taken much longer than Al had anticipated. Everything had just been so far apart, by Al's reckoning. And then when they'd gotten there, the parking lot had been a bloated monstrosity. Joan tried to get them moving at speed, leading the way toward the soulless edifice of Byers Arena.

15

CARDINAL CHINS

As JOAN first gazed through the glass doors, she felt uneasy. In a way, the building should have felt comfortable for her, since she'd spent a great deal of time locked in castles, not to mention working in the massive and uncomfortable structure at The Institute at the Beginning of Time. But Byers Arena had uncanny white walls, artificial light, and stairways so wide no knight could hope to hold them. The longer she gazed, the more certain she became: Byers Arena was a death trap. Nevertheless, without a thought of turning back, she walked toward the entrance.

Once through the spinning doors, Joan stopped in her tracks. If she'd been a train, she might have derailed then and there. As it was, she barely avoided colliding with her own caboose.

The last time Joan was this surprised, she had been a captive in a dismal castle in the town of Rouen. Not that the castle itself was particularly dismal, merely that even the most luxurious accommodations available were rather uncomfortable, and Joan was hardly in the most luxurious of accommodations. She was suffering the hospitality of Henry VI. He'd just come into possession of quite a few lovely countryside estates—wonderful examples of the latest motte-and-bailey style—and after washing away the blood and pacifying the peasantry, he was eager to host some of the neighbors for an extended stay. It was a period of terror for the peasants of Normandy, and even worse for Joan, who was not only imprisoned but charged with heresy. Her outlook couldn't have gotten much worse. It was the eve of her execution, and she was locked in a dingy room deep within a sinister castle, and smack in the middle of occupied France during the horror of the Hundred Years' War.

Still, the battle-hardened veteran was flabbergasted when a clean-cut man strode into her cell. She was expecting one of the cruel and detestable guards to walk in, not a graceful young man in an immaculate, if unflattering, blue unitard. Luckily, he had the figure to pull it off. Joan had never seen anything like his clothing. Her first thought was that he was wearing vestments. Was it silk, from the distant east? Was it velvet, imported from Timbuktu? Only the church had access to such extravagant luxuries. The same church that had imprisoned her and charged her with heresy.

It was only natural that Joan assumed the handsome man in the soft blue pajamas was a clergyman. And despite—or perhaps because of—her intense religiosity, Joan did not get on well with priests. The whole trial-for-heresy thing hadn't helped one bit with her opinion of organized religion, so she really wasn't very happy to see him.

Still, the stranger had an angular, reassuring face. It was a handsome face. It was the kind of face that would in later years be used with great effect to market safety razors. His hair was close-cropped. His manner was professional and forthright. His muscles were so well defined they could be used in a sentence.

As soon as he saw Joan sitting on her straw pallet, he froze. His eyes widened, and he gave a short and quiet squeal of surprise. "You're avake?" he asked her.

"So I presume," she said, though now she was beginning to wonder.

Embarrassment spilled across his face. "You are Joan, are you not?"

"I am she," Joan admitted.

"Good, good. At least I'm . . ." He looked around the cell and remembered himself. "Forgive me. Where are my manners? I'm Manfred von Richthofen." He clicked his heels together and gave her a curt nod.

"Pardon me?" Joan said. At once she felt embarrassed by her inarticulacy. In fact, she was confident that if she'd even tried to pronounce 'inarticulacy,' her tongue would revolt and make its own way down her throat.

The pajama-clad clergyman paid it no heed. "It's a pleasure to meet you, madam."

Joan looked around the squalid cell. "Is it?" she asked. She cringed at herself. *What wit!* Far easier to make a quip than to ask for mercy.

"It is. I assure you." He took in the condition of her cell with dismay. "Though the circumstances leave much to be desired."

Joan blinked. She hadn't been expecting kindness. "Then be welcome," she said, determined to match the stranger's gentility. "I can offer neither wine nor meat, only what meager fare my captors allow me."

"Quite generous of you, madam, but I must decline." He smiled. "I had a large lunch, anyway."

"I see," Joan said, inexplicably disappointed.

For a long moment neither spoke, though their eyes caught. Manfred looked away, a blush rising to his cheeks.

"I should be off," Manfred said, making no move to leave.

"Oh?" she asked.

"Yes," he continued with regret. "This has been a most unfortunate mistake."

"There have been many errors of late," Joan noted.

"My sincerest apologies," Manfred added. "I must go." Still he made no move toward the exit.

"As you say."

"By the by," Manfred began offhandedly, "what day is today?"

"Saturday," Joan said. She would die on the Sabbath.

"Well, that explains it. Another cock-up." He pulled out the timepiece he wore around his neck and examined it closely.

"Cock-up?" Joan asked, fascinated with the dials and knobs on the extravagant pocket watch. It looked like just the kind of thing a priest would wear.

"Sorry." Manfred stuffed his timepiece back down his shirt. "I meant only to say, that I was supposed to arrive tomorrow."

"You're early."

"That's about the sum of it."

Joan settled wearily. "Have you come to interrogate me?"

"No, no." Manfred waved his arms dramatically. "Nothing like that," he assured her pleasantly.

Joan sighed. "Torture, then?" She unlimbered herself.

"I should say not!" he protested. "I would never torture a . . ." He gestured vaguely to Joan. "Anyone. Besides, torture? Aren't they killing you tomorrow? Why bother to—"

"Then you will assist me with my last rites?" Joan pressed. Considering she was being held for heresy, her hosts had shown remarkably little interest in their religious duties.

"Ach. No," Manfred said with regret. He shook his fists in mock anger. "I'm afraid not. That wouldn't be prudent. I don't think I'd get it right, anyway."

"Why not?" Joan asked, not used to humility from the clergy.

"Well, I'm a Lutheran, for one," Manfred explained.

"Lutheran?" Joan asked.

Manfred sighed. "That is to say, a Protestant," he clarified.

Joan raised an eyebrow. "What do you protest?"

"No, that's not what it means." Manfred squinted at her suspiciously. "You'd think The Watch would prevent . . ." He looked around and sighed. "A Protestant is, well . . ." He sat on the far side of her pallet and rubbed his hands together thoughtfully. "You see, this gentleman named Luther came along, und he hammered a list of complaints on a church door. He was rather unhappy with the Catholics. Or at least he was quite upset with the priests."

Joan glared into the distance, lost in a memory. "I know just how he felt."

"You do?" Manfred snorted with amusement. "Of course! You do." He chuckled to himself. "Of course."

"What was on Sir Luther's list?" Joan prompted.

"Oh, rather a lot, really," Manfred hedged.

Joan smiled. "I can think of a few things myself."

"I'm sure you can."

Joan waited for further clarification, but he told her no specifics. Eventually she asked, "If you are not a priest, then why are you wearing vestments?"

"This?" He looked down at the blue unitard. "Gott in . . . another screwup. I didn't set this thing properly. It was meant to look like a peasant's smock."

"A smock?" she asked, bewildered.

"You know," Manfred said, struggling for an explanation. "Sort of a loose-fitting shirt. Not very fashionable, but it was supposed to, supposed to . . ."

"What is it?" Joan asked, aware of his sudden discomfort.

"I shouldn't be saying any of this," he added, blinking and squinting as realization dawned.

"Why not?" she pressed, even more eager for an answer.

Manfred scratched his well-shaped chin. "Well, the most important thing is, I was supposed to arrive on Sunday."

"I'll be killed on Sunday," Joan pointed out.

"Indeed," Manfred said with a sour little laugh.

Joan frowned. "You came to see me die."

"I've already said too much," Manfred admitted. "I cannot tell you any more."

Joan almost felt sorry for him. "Then why do you keep talking?"

"It's just that I become nervous when I'm around beautiful women." He reddened. "Which is not so often anymore, not with a war on."

"I see," Joan said. The compliment wasn't completely disagreeable.

"Not that there's a war on, anymore," Manfred added. "Not to say that there ever will be. Or won't be."

"There is most certainly a war." Joan closed her eyes for a terrible instant. "I've seen quite a few battles."

"Well, yes. You have. There's a war on now, but not later. I mean, there will be again, of course. I missed the end of mine." His attempts to explain were only confusing her further. "I'm rather sticking my foot in it again, aren't I?"

"In what?" Joan asked, growing somewhat tired of the man's inscrutability.

"It's . . . look." He was wringing his hands. "You're just going to have to forget that you ever saw me."

Joan raised her eyebrows. "Forget?" she asked.

He nodded. "In a manner of speaking. It's not like I'm going to cosh you on the back of the head or anything, und you'll wake up wondering if I was a dream." He waved away the idea. "Not that it works like that. The cosh I mean. It's not brain surgery."

"I didn't say—"

"It's a blunt instrument inducing massive brain damage," Manfred continued. "No real room for local amnesia in there."

"I won't forget this," she warned.

"Certainly not. That's not . . ." Manfred took a slow breath and resolved to get back on track. "You don't actually have to forget, but you can't tell anyone."

Joan eyed him with even more suspicion. "Who would I tell?"

"The guards. The executioner. Or maybe whoever does come around to see about the last rites."

"And why shouldn't I tell them?" Joan asked, a dangerous edge in her voice.

"It'd rather upset all of our plans, wouldn't it?" Manfred asked with the hint of a smile.

"I have none," Joan reminded him.

"That's good," Manfred said flippantly. "You won't be here long."

"Charming."

"Wait! I've got it." Manfred practically giggled, his delight was so palpable. "Oh, this is perfect."

"Got what?" Joan asked, looking around.

"I'm an angel," Manfred said, with a cherubic grin.

"An angel? I do not think you are an angel." Joan began to wonder if this had all been a ruse to catch her in a heresy.

"An angel from heaven," Manfred added.

"And, my so-called angel, why are you here?"

"I'm here . . ." Manfred clicked his tongue as he thought. "I'm here to tell you to have faith! Have faith. That's it. Faith that everything will turn out okay in the end. Und Gott! Have faith in Gott, too, of course. That goes without saying, I should think. Und now I'm off." Manfred nodded with satisfaction and assurance. "You won't be seeing any more of me, at least until tomorrow."

"What happens tomorrow?" Joan asked, more confused than ever.

"They'll be killing you, won't they?" he asked, oblivious to Joan's dismay. "Unless I've totally upended the timeline here. But I shouldn't have. Not if you don't say anything." As if to enlist her help, he gave her a conspiratorial wink.

It was a terrible wink. The Interdimensional Society of Winkers would name it one of the ten worst winks in the multiverse. It would go on to hold a spot on the top-ten list for centuries, until Pope Kanye III suffered a minor stroke mid-eulogy, the highlight of a funeral to commemorate the first—and last—attempt at an unassisted solo ascent of Mons Olympus.

"Why shouldn't I say anything?" Joan asked. She was thoroughly unconvinced by the wink, which, as mentioned, was almost as bad as a pope's inadvertent twitching during a galactically televised funeral.

"You've got to have faith, for one," Manfred added,

somehow sensing that his wink alone hadn't quite sealed the deal. "I mentioned that, didn't I?"

"Yes, you did."

"All right, then." He nodded to himself again. "It's Gott's plan, I'd say."

"My death? That's God's plan?"

"You've got it. Take comfort." A modest smile tried to take root on his face, but skittered away, carrying with it his failing confidence. "Good, good," Manfred added weakly. "All right, well. I'm off."

"Take me with you," Joan said quietly. It was the most she had asked for herself since she'd been a child. Making the request was terribly difficult. "Please."

"Ah." Regret and dismay played across Manfred's face. "I'm afraid I cannot."

Joan snorted and turned aside. "Another coward." She shouldn't have bothered to ask for help.

"It is not that, I assure you." He took a single step toward her and stopped himself reluctantly.

"You lack the courage to save me from the fire," she accused him.

"If only I could, madam," Manfred assured her. "I would whisk you away to eternity."

For a moment she almost believed him. His jaw was extremely chiseled, she noted again, although why it should matter, she couldn't quite remember. "Perhaps it is right that I should be condemned for wearing a man's clothes. I am more of a man than you."

"You may be right." It seemed as if he was going to say more. Then Manfred shook his head and looked sideways at the door.

"Farewell, brave Manfred," Joan told him.

"Ta-ta," he said. His regret was almost immediate. One of the greatest ironies a time traveler endured was the inability to go back and rectify an embarrassing mistake. He would live with the stark and uncompromising memory of that "ta-ta" until the day he died. Again.

"I shall bear your tidings with fortitude and faith," Joan assured him.

"Oh, well, that's good. That's just . . ." He blinked, and then turned that surprisingly charming smile on Joan. "Wish I'd thought of that. That's a good way to put it. Anyhoo, I'm off."

"You said that," Joan pointed out, growing somehow amused at his fluster.

Manfred's smile slipped away. "I did, didn't I?"

Joan grinned at his discomfiture. "A few times, now."

Manfred made for the exit. "Well, third time's the charm. Have faith und all that! I'm off. Really this time." He closed the door behind him, sliding the bar back into place with a clank.

That was the last she'd seen of the man in the blue unitard. The next day, it was a different fellow entirely who plucked her away from the pyre just as she felt the tickle of that terrible flame on the soles of her feet.

So, it was rather a shock to Joan that six hundred years later, half a world away, she should spot the same clean-cut gentleman in the lobby of the Byers Arena. He was moving quite fast through the wide corridor, away from her, as if with some urgent purpose. It was him, she was sure of it.

Before the strange man could slip away into the crowd, Joan was after him.

No one saw her go.

16

CONVENTIONAL DRESS

WHILE JOAN WAS CHASING A FALLEN angel from her past, Al was having a similarly jarring experience. Al had been recognized.

One might think that an organization as resourceful as The Institute at the Beginning of Time would have a procedure in place if one of their operatives was recognized, particularly given The Institute's tendency to send operatives to assignments close to their own time.

Truthfully, there was one researcher, Amos, who did foresee the problem. He wrote quite a convincing memo about it, eight pages in total, in twelve-point font and everything, and sent it with a subject reading *"URGENT"* to a mailing list including most of his colleagues in the Department of Procedure, all of the Senior Advisory Committee, the Executive Board, the Board of Directors, and the Steering Committee. He'd even found an old routing address for Professor Filigree and went ahead and sent him the memo as well.

He sent the memo to so many people, in fact, that no one thought it was actually addressed to them. Everyone thought they were being updated on someone else's business.

Not a single person had replied to his memo, and Amos slowly realized that his warning had gone entirely unnoticed.

The incident prompted Amos to write a second memo, this one describing the previous incident, and proposing new procedures for the dispersion of memos. This time the subject read "FREE CUPCAKES" and he sent it to only two people: Frank, his immediate supervisor, and the Director of the Department of Procedure, who was also named Frank. The proposal was accepted and enacted within a month. Amos was promoted within a year. Decades later, Amos would publicly credit that memo for his own eventual appointment to the Directorship of the Department of Procedure. Of course, by then, even Amos had forgotten about the whole time-traveling-agents-being-recognized thing. Despite finally having the authority to do something about it, Amos too neglected the problem. He spent his twilight years crafting a new departmental manual on revisions, and he never really got around to anything else.

The lack of procedure in cases of recognition still

shouldn't have been a problem for Al: There weren't that many people around who would actually remember him. There was his mother, of course, and his uncle Ned. Though Ned wasn't really his uncle, and unbeknownst to Al, his name wasn't really Ned.

There was also the lady down the hall in his apartment building—Dr. Edith Warner in 311, though Al always thought of her as "the lady down the hall"—who was increasingly irate about the bicycle Al sometimes left in the corridor. Two years and three new neighbors later, and still his bicycle remained chained to the railing. She wasn't going to forget him, not ever.

Nor was "Uncle Ned" likely to recognize him, having left the vicinity of Oakland shortly after Al's funeral. Though Al had no way of knowing, his mother Myrtle wasn't around either, on account of her terrible grief over Al's death. In fact, she'd been so distraught over the loss of her son that shortly after his death she'd said goodbye to her bridge club and moved to Reno. Myrtle had chosen Reno because the desert landscape matched the barren condition of her heart, and also because it was legal to play blackjack there.

As a result, very few people might actually recognize Al, and be surprised to see him, despite the fact that he had only traveled two years into the future and one hundred fifty miles from his old apartment. There were a few former coworkers from Lower Midlands Advertising who would know him, if not by name, then by face.

Ironically, Al had a very recognizable face. This was not because of its features, which were on the whole quite unremarkable, but because of the expression he often wore. It was an expression of weary resignation. It was the look of a search engine optimization specialist whose suggestions for optimization were invariably ignored and unheeded. It was similar to the look on a dentist's face when he or she reminded a patient to floss twice daily.

Al wore his expression of weary resignation at that very moment, which may have been why Lily from Legal recognized him in the first place.

"Al?" she cried out in shock.

Everything would have turned out differently if Al had simply ignored her cry. Lily would have screwed up her eyes, shaken her head, and chalked the whole thing up to a phantom brought on by post-traumatic stress from hiding in a closet while a coworker was shot.

Al, like pretty much everyone else for thousands of years, had been conditioned from birth to respond to people calling out his name. So when Lily cried out, "Al!" he turned to her and said, "Yes?" without much thought.

This casual response was almost as strange to Lily as the reappearance of the presumably dead Al.

Al and Lily stared at each other in silence for quite a long time. Neither wanted to be first to speak. The social etiquette of running into a dead coworker was a surprisingly tricky thing, and Lily was rather put off. Al spent a great deal of thought on why he hadn't anticipated running into anyone he knew. Then he spent even more time and energy regretting that he was disguised as a pizza delivery guy in short shorts.

"I thought you were dead," Lily eventually told him.

"Technically, I am," Al admitted.

"That's not funny."

Al nodded. "Would you believe it if I said I wasn't me?"

Lily arched her eyebrow. "Not anymore."

"That ship has sailed," he said ruefully, looking around desperately for a life preserver.

"I'd say so." Lily took a close look at his pizza delivery hat, and his pizza delivery jacket. She wondered where the pizza was.

"How was my funeral?" Al asked. A moment later he cringed. It was the most awkward attempt at small talk since a passenger on the Lusitania had asked if anyone else fancied a swim.

"I . . ." She looked away.

"That bad?" Al asked. "Did the casket fall to the ground or something?"

"No." Lily shook her head. She seemed almost embarrassed.

"You didn't go," Al guessed.

She shrugged. "It was bad timing for me."

"Bad timing? No, no. It's my fault. I'm sorry I didn't take your weekend plans into account when I was shot in the head."

"My cousin was visiting from Sacramento," she explained.

"I wouldn't want to interfere with a visit from faraway Sacramento," Al said with derision.

"You're not upset, are you?"

"I can't say I'm happy about it," Al said, his arms akimbo.

"But you're not even dead," she pointed out. "You can't be angry I skipped your funeral when you're not even dead."

"I was dead," he assured her. "I'm just not dead anymore."

"If anything, you should be apologizing for letting all of us think you were dead!"

"Yeah, it seems like you were quite broken up about it."

"We canceled casual Friday," Lily offered, pursing her lips.

"What a sacrifice."

Lily frowned. "I like casual Friday."

"Everybody likes casual Friday," Al said bitterly. "That's the whole point of it."

"Not that week. It was dreadful. We met in the break-room and shared our favorite memories of the victims."

"That's something."

"It was very touching. Martha from HR was bawling."

"Martha?"

"Yes."

"But Martha hated me," Al said, remembering a bevy of inappropriate aphorisms.

"She was sobbing."

"She would, wouldn't she." Despite himself, Al felt a smile form at the corner of his mouth.

"Even Phillip teared up."

"Phillip!" He was shocked. And also, somehow offended.

"Not a dry eye in the room."

"That's something, at least." Al took great comfort in their grief.

"Listen, how is it that you're"—she gestured vaguely in his direction—"you know."

"Alive?" he suggested, demonstrating with a stretch.

Lily cocked her head. "Not to put too fine a point on it."

Al nodded thoughtfully. "What about Witness Protection? Would you believe I'm in Witness Protection?" Al asked. He wasn't very good at thinking on his feet. He was also fairly lousy at thinking while seated.

"They didn't move you very far, did they?" Lily said. Though the Legal Department at Lower Midlands Advertising rarely dealt with the Witness Protection program, Lily felt certain she was right on this one.

"Give me a minute and I'll come up with something," Al said, holding up a finger.

"Al, I need to know the truth," Lily pressed. "You can't go pretending you've died. What happened?"

"The trouble is I can't tell you."

"You won't answer even a single question!"

"I want to tell you the truth," Al said. "I want to tell you everything, but something is preventing me."

Lily snorted. "You sound like my college boyfriend." Al indeed sounded remarkably like her old flame.

Lily's beau, although a perfectly nice guy otherwise, had claimed to be haunted by the ghost of his paternal grandmother, who would regularly terrorize him for not dating a fellow Catholic. As a consequence, he entirely avoided discussing the subject of dating so as to keep from offending the spirit and invoking her wrath. Eventually his refusal to acknowledge their relationship verbally became a sore point for Lily.

Al, though completely ignorant of the haunted boyfriend incident, could nonetheless tell that his lack of explanation hadn't placated Lily. "You don't understand," Al objected. "If I say anything, all Hell could break loose." Al still, in fact, sounded remarkably like Lily's old boyfriend.

"Then explain it to me," she said, through a smile suspiciously sweet.

"I could be risking the entire course of history, or something," he muttered halfheartedly.

"You think that makes me less interested?" Lily cocked her head. "What the hell happened?"

Al had quite a few choices at this juncture. He could have lied. He could have refused to answer. He might have redirected the line of questioning or challenged the assumptions of the question. He could have pretended he was under attack by an invisible monster and promptly run away or even distracted everyone with a shiny metal gadget.

Al did exactly none of those things: Al told the truth. "I'm a time traveler. All right? Happy? I'm a goddamn time traveler." No sooner had he finished speaking than he regretted his choice. He felt in his pockets for anything shiny and metallic, wondering if he'd waited too long already.

"You're from the future," Lily repeated incredulously. It didn't appear that she was going to be purchasing the daily special.

"No," he said slowly, "not exactly."

"Then where . . . when are you from?" she asked.

"I've traveled a vast distance through time and space, and learned many terrible things."

"How far have you come?"

"At this point I'm two years into the future," Al said, quickly amending, "but I did make a stop on the way."

Lily couldn't follow. "But I was with you two years ago!"

"Yes, but I wasn't around for all the days in between." Al looked around for his backup, and saw they'd wandered toward the convention hall. He began to inch in their direction.

"Then where were you?" Lily asked in exasperation.

"When," Al said obtusely, looking over his shoulder.

"When what?"

"When was I."

"When were you what?" Lily said, throwing her hands in the air.

"That's it exactly," Al said. He was just happy someone finally understood him.

Lily wondered if the whole story was worth the effort of disbelieving. "This is very confusing," she said to herself. Al couldn't help but overhear.

He nodded. "Then you're definitely starting to get the picture." In Al's experience, if comprehension ever came, it was after a great deal of stumbling around and latching onto various sharp projections.

"Why are *you* here?" he asked, hoping to put her on the back foot.

"I grew up here."

"In the arena? Were your parents in the circus?"

"In Fresno. I'm only at the arena to—" She caught herself. "Don't change the subject. You've been time traveling for the past two years, and you've only just gotten back to the present, where—"

"The future," Al interjected.

"What do you mean, 'the future'?"

"This," Al said, gesturing around them. "This is the future."

Lily looked around suspiciously. "It seems like the present."

"It always seems like the present, doesn't it?" Al pointed out.

"I don't see any flying cars," Lily said. To be fair, she wasn't really looking for any.

"Don't be silly."

"No robots," she added.

"He was here a minute ago," Al said, once again looking over his shoulder.

"Who was?" she said, craning to see just what Al was looking at.

"The robot," Al said, now facing completely away from Lily and eyeing the distant crowd.

"Al," she said in a quiet, resigned voice, "you've really lost it."

"Him," Al said, eyes darting around the foyer. "I've lost *him*." Suddenly Al was very concerned for HCL. There was no telling what that cyborg would do on his own.

Attempting to reproduce with a video game console wasn't entirely implausible.

"Him?" Lily asked, interrupting his rumination.

"The robot's a man," Al clarified. There was still no sign of him.

"The robot's a man?" Lily repeated, growing exasperated.

Al nodded. "That's right. Actually, he's a cyborg." Al stroked his bare chin. "Is the cyborg the one with the meat parts?"

"That is correct," HCL said as he approached.

"There he is!" Al said, hurrying over to HCL. "I wasn't worried one bit. Oh, I'm sorry." He turned to include Lily. "HCL, this is Lily. Lily, this is HCL."

"A pleasure," Lily said. It was in no way a pleasure, but humans of the early twenty-first century made a great deal of meaningless statements. If Lily had been at a party, this would have been the point when she excused herself to go looking for some crudités or tiny sandwiches.

"This is the cyborg I was telling you about," Al prompted her.

"You expect me to believe this firefighter is a cyborg?" Lily asked.

"Yes," Al answered. Almost immediately he began to contradict himself: "Actually just a firefighter!"

"Right," HCL said, nodding sagely. "A *human* firefighter." The cyborg walked away, feeling he'd really sold it.

Lily knew exactly what to believe. Nothing. "I can't listen to this."

"Sure." Al nodded dumbly. He added, "I get that."

Fortunately for Al, the sudden appearance of a towering nun grimacing from beneath her wimple interrupted his display of rapidly deteriorating conversational acumen.

"Who's this?" Impala asked suspiciously.

Al cleared his throat. "Lily, this is Impala. Impala, Lily."

Lily eyed her up and down, taking in the habit and wimple. "I hope you're here to take him back to the hospital, sister," Lily said.

Impala spent a moment sizing Lily up. For Impala, sizing someone up meant deciding on the quickest way to kill them. She zeroed in quickly on Lily's useless V-neck shirt and the fragile neck it revealed. Once she'd thought of a few possibilities, Impala said, "I'm a nun."

Lily blinked. "Yes, I can see that."

"She's not really a nun," Al quickly said.

Impala cast an angry glance at him. "I am a nun." She gestured to her habit. "See?"

"She's joking," Al mumbled to Lily.

"Don't blow our cover!" Impala remonstrated.

"It's not a cover," Al told Lily. Then he pleaded, "Hold on just a minute."

"We need to go." Impala pulled on his arm.

Al shook her off. "I'd like just a moment to talk here, this might be my last—"

"Are the three of you here for the convention?" Lily asked, in a commendable effort to change the subject. When she wanted, her small talk would elicit no criticism, comment, or even thought. She was quite good at it.

The convention. Al gulped. "Please, Lily, promise me you'll leave here at once," Al said, now sounding much like a temperance worker. "Under no circumstances go near the convention."

"I was only here to pick up tickets at the box office."

Al shook his head. "Going to the convention could cost you your life."

"I wouldn't be caught dead there anyway," Lily assured him.

"What?" Al asked. "Why?"

HCL ran across the foyer and back to the group, announcing, "We must find a fortified location. There is a large group of extraterrestrials headed this way."

"They'll just have to . . ." The import of the sentence worked its way into the forefront of Al's mind. Then it began jumping up and down and shouting. "What do you mean? Aliens?"

"Aliens. At least a dozen, of multiple species. Two of them were visibly armed."

"Armed?" Al said in alarm.

"They're here for the Fresno M.E.D. Convention." Lily pointed into the arena. "Just down the hall."

"Why would aliens attend a medical convention?" Al asked.

"I don't mean to alarm anyone," HCL said slowly. "But they appear to be carrying some type of portable phase cannon that could, conceivably, wipe all life from the face of the planet."

"It's not a medical convention," Lily said, with frightening certainty. "It's a Man Eats Dragon Convention," she explained, edging toward the exit. "It's like a postmodern take on fantasy and sci-fi—all of the camp, none of the earnestness." She'd almost made it to the door.

Al turned, and got his first look at the aliens.

Cosplayers. Dozens of them. "They're costumes," he muttered. "They're all in costumes."

17

A TEACHABLE TORMENT

In the depths of the Byers Arena, every aspect of twenty-first-century mythology was cavorting together in the air-conditioning. Al, by way of contrast, was escorting a pair of trigger-happy time travelers through a reality fully adulterated by the imaginary.

A science-fiction convention, he mused. Perhaps the most confusing and treacherous ground a team of time travelers could enter. The other timekeepers would find themselves unable to distinguish truth from lies, or pretense from irony. *It might as well be a hall of mirrors. They'll be lost without me.* The realization was a bitter draught.

"I need you both to listen very closely," Al said, lowering his voice.

"What is it, fellow hominid?" asked HCL, moving closer. "We have very little time before the extraterrestrials become aware of our position. I doubt their interaction with that sausage vendor will distract them for long."

"Spill it." Impala shouldered in.

Al took a deep breath. "Those 'aliens' with the guns aren't real. They're people in costumes." Al held up his hand to keep them from interrupting. "What you're about to see," he went on, "is a science-fiction convention. None of it is real. The place we're going to . . ." He staggered to the edge of the cultural canyon between them and looked down in despair. "It's like a costume party."

"They're uniforms," Impala muttered.

"No, these are costumes," Al insisted patiently.

"He's lost it," Impala whispered. "More of it."

"No." Al thought the Almanac should have made this type of confusion impossible. "Please try to understand for a moment: This is a science-fiction convention." He pointed at the mad circus down the hall.

"What is?" Impala asked.

"Everything over there," Al said, gesturing widely. "The people are wearing costumes. They're pretending to be aliens, or knights, or people from the future, or superheroes, or stuff like that." What was he missing? "They're doing it for fun. Do you understand?"

"Not at all," Impala said.

"You can't trust what you're seeing here!" he shouted. "We had it all wrong!"

"I wonder if there are any psychologists at the convention," Impala said to HCL. "We could use some help."

"Nonsense," HCL said. "I'm a more capable doctor than any of these primitive hominids."

"Forget the doctors!" Al shouted. "There are no doctors, understand? Not one. And you need to prepare yourself for a whole new reality."

"I have a sedative prepared," HCL noted to Impala.

Impala shrugged. "I'm not going to carry him."

"No! You have to listen to me," Al pleaded. Judging by the sudden appearance of the needle, HCL had been hiding a syringe within his left index finger. "You have to rely on my judgment." Impala was stretching her shoulders like a great cat unlimbering. "Both of you, calm down a bit. Ease up. That's it." He went to put his hand on Impala's arm but thought better of it: She was looking at his neck with a strange intensity again.

Suddenly Impala snarled and pushed down hard on Al's shoulder. He stumbled to the floor. Impala was off, bounding down the corridor with one incredible leap after another. *What the hell?* Al frantically looked for whatever had triggered Impala's response.

HCL took one step after her and stopped himself, waiting as the needle slowly retracted back into his finger.

Impala's intentions became more clear when she picked up the stanchion holding a velvet rope and began to swing it around her head, readying for an attack. It all came into focus when Al saw the figure beyond her: a cosplayer dressed as a werewolf. The innocent—if poorly costumed—lycanthrope was making his way toward the convention, stopping every few steps to adjust his outfit.

"No!" Al shouted, running toward her.

Impala stalked forward. She raised high the post.

"Stop!" Al shouted as he collided with Impala, the two of them knocking into the cosplayer and falling in an ungainly pile of stanchion and velvet ropes. "That's a man in a werewolf costume!" Al shouted, trying to protect his kidneys. "Not a wolf, all right? Not a werewolf!" The pile beneath him was no longer struggling. Neither was he, come to think of it. Some sort of detente having been reached between them, he helped Impala to her feet.

The collision had knocked the mask off the werewolf's head. The very human-looking man within glared at them.

"It looked like a monster," Impala said, reluctantly accepting that the furry stranger was a pudgy man in a felt costume.

Al waved away her concern, trying to catch his breath. "I'll give you a signal if we're actually in any danger."

"What signal?" Impala asked.

Thinking at a moderate pace, if not exactly quickly, Al told her, "I'll scream."

"That will be sufficient." HCL nodded, approaching. "While the two of you were wrestling, I happened to notice that Joan has disappeared."

Al turned to him. "What do you mean, 'disappeared'?"

Impala was on her feet at once, tapping on her phone. "She's not responding on comms."

"I can't pinpoint the location of her Almanac on my scanner," HCL added.

"She's probably in the bathroom or something." Al spun around. "Where is she?"

"We don't know!" Impala shouted. She and HCL shared a look. "Haven't you heard a word I've said?"

"No, Lily, the woman I was just . . ." Al spun around fruitlessly. "She's gone."

"Huh." Impala took a casual glance around. "Both of them disappearing at the same time. Something's not right about this Lily character. Want me to track her down and kill her?"

Al was dumbfounded. "No! Why would you kill her?"

"We have to protect the timeline," Impala told him with a shrug.

"Killing a bystander from the twenty-first century would totally foul up the timeline, wouldn't it?" asked Al.

"Only one way to find out." She rubbed her hands together.

"We could consult the Almanac's historical databanks," Al suggested.

"Oh," Impala frowned. "That would work. Two ways."

"Or have HCL run some simulations," Al added.

"Three ways." Impala flexed.

"We could ask the—"

"You made your point, before-timer," Impala told him forcefully.

"Let's not jump into a confrontation," Al counseled. "There's going to be hundreds of them in there. Were-wolves, and aliens, and monsters. All of it." He looked from HCL to Impala with concern. "Are you ready to trust me? If you want to find Joan, you're going to have to trust me."

"He didn't smell like a wolf," Impala noted.

"And he wasn't a wolf," Al agreed. "Just keep smelling, then. I'm not any good at it."

Impala nodded. "I smell enough for all of us."

"I . . ." Al shrugged. "Let's find Joan," he continued, leading them deeper into the arena. "We've only got a few minutes before we need to get into position." Al grimaced, contemplating the grim and unwelcome task before them— they were here to protect the timeline, after all. "I suggest we split up and meet back here in five minutes. HCL, you check the parking lot. I'll get the corridors. And Impala, you search the women's restroom."

"I'm not checking the restroom," Impala growled.

Al saw Impala's expression just in time to stifle his laughter. "If someone needs to check the women's restroom," he said gently, "it has to be you."

"No," she said. It was the first time Al had seen Impala look so disturbed. "I'm not risking it."

"Risking what?" Al asked, wondering what could scare

a woman as fierce and fearsome as Impala of House Chevrolet.

"Did you check the Almanac's entry on public restrooms?" she asked warily.

No sooner had Impala reminded him of the Almanac, than the soothing voice manifested inside his consciousness.

"Public restrooms in the twenty-first century present a terribly sticky business. Due to the intricacy of customs and the severe consequences for inappropriate behavior, the time traveler is urged simply to hold it whenever possible. If a public restroom must be used, the time traveler should enter any empty stall, lock the door, and do their best to pretend that no one can see or hear them, or vice versa, for as long as is necessary to indulge their bodily functions. Under no circumstances whatsoever should any time traveler approach a urinal: The effort and time saved in such an attempt must be weighed against the likelihood of disaster and ruin, and in every case found severely wanting.

"After one's business is done, proceed immediately to the sink without making eye contact. Perform the most perfunctory washing of hands,

being sure to splash a small amount of water on one's pants while quietly saying "damn it" or "not again." At this point—but not before!—the time-keeper may establish eye contact with those near the sinks, so long as it is accompanied by a rueful shake of the head."

"That's all a bit overblown," Al told Impala.

"A bit?" she asked.

"Well," he relented, "it's right about the eye-contact thing. Nobody walks around a public restroom actually making eye contact."

"And the . . ." She looked around as if something might be sneaking up on them. "The 'urinals'?"

"I wouldn't suggest you try one," Al said. "But there won't be any in the—"

"I'm not going in there," Impala growled.

"It will be fine," Al assured her.

"I'm not even wearing pants," Impala said.

"You don't need pants," Al pointed out. "You're wearing a habit."

"If you would like me to sedate her, just give the word," HCL offered eagerly.

"Shut up," she snapped at the cyborg. "You're not sedating me."

"You've got to do it, for Joan," Al pointed out. "And for the timeline! You're the only one who—"

"Fine," Impala snarled. "If I'm not back in five minutes . . ." Her voice caught in her throat.

"Yes?" Al asked.

She shuddered. "Send the cyborg after me."

"It's a deal," Al told her.

Impala crept into the public restroom and out of their sight with the care and purpose of a panther on the prowl.

HCL ran to the front entrance to case out the parking lot.

Al jogged down the nearest corridor.

Five minutes later, HCL and Al returned to the agreed-upon spot, each empty-handed.

"Is Impala usually late for things?" Al asked, tapping at his Almanac, still camouflaged as a nifty smartwatch. "She said five minutes."

"That is unnecessary," HCL said. "I'm utilizing my internal chronometer."

"Handy thing to have," Al said. Al tapped his foot. Then he tapped his hand. Then he spoke. "Something's been bothering me," he said to HCL.

HCL nodded and let out a long sigh. "Is it the contempt I have for ancient hominids such as yourself?"

"No, I . . ." Al frowned. "You hold me in contempt?"

"Why do you ask?" HCL replied.

"You just said it," said Al. "You said you held me in contempt."

"I was only trying to guess the source of your discomfort," HCL stated. "I apologize for any offense I may have caused. Please continue."

Al shuffled his feet. "What's been bothering me—"

"You've worked out that you have no useful role on this mission," HCL interjected. "That you are, to be blunt, dead weight." HCL was scanning their environs, not even bothering to look Al in the eyes as he delivered his withering dismissal.

"No! I think I've been doing a bang-up job."

"In your opinion," HCL added.

"I . . ." Al swallowed and nodded. "Yes. In my opinion. What's really bothering me—"

"Is it that you've realized—"

"Stop!" Al shouted. Any more of this and he would have to take HCL up on his offer for psychiatric treatment. "Just let me get to the goddamn point."

"Please, proceed," HCL said. "I wouldn't want to cause you any distress."

"Really?" Al asked.

"Of course," HCL assured him. "Distressed hominids make very annoying noises."

"You said that in your time, accidental death had been all but wiped out," Al began, "that planned obsolescence was the main cause of an individual's demise."

HCL nodded sagely. "And this distresses you because you realize that your own death is—on a cosmic level—a mere blink of an eye away."

"You must be fun at parties."

"I am rarely invited to parties," HCL said.

"I wonder why."

"I too am unable to understand the oversight."

"Let's circle back to that," said Al, picturing a very large circle. "But with accidental and violent death virtually a thing of the past . . ." Aloysius paused, waiting for HCL's inevitable interruption.

"Please continue."

"Yes." Al nodded. "Of course. The Institute only recruits those whose untimely deaths were recorded in the historical record."

"An accurate assessment."

"So how did you die?" Al asked.

For a brief moment, Al thought he saw an expression of regret on HCL's face.

"That is a source of embarrassment," HCL said.

"Embarrassment?" Al scoffed. "From a cyborg?"

"As a cyborg, I experience the full range of human emotions. I simply have a superior faculty for suppressing them."

"Like a Vulcan!" Al said, smiling.

"What?" HCL asked.

"Like Spock." Al waited, but no response came from

HCL. "You know, Spock? I could have sworn I mentioned him earlier."

"I am unfamiliar with that reference."

"You know Gort, but not Spock?" Al asked.

HCL shrugged. "Gort was a hero. His timely intervention in Earth's history will never be forgotten."

"Wait. Are you under the impression that . . ." Al sighed. "It doesn't matter."

"As you say. Compared to a planetary hero such as Gort, we are unimportant. Regardless, my death is not an event I like to dwell on."

Al could relate. "Tell me about it," he commiserated.

"No," the cyborg replied. But it was too late. HCL's inability to recognize a rhetorical question had already brought an unpleasant memory to the forefront of his mind.

18

THE DANGERS OF DOXING

THE IMPORTANT THING TO remember is that HCL had been young. Not young by Al's twenty-first-century standards, and certainly not young by the standards of Impala or Joan, both of them having grown up without significant medical care. But HCL was young by the standards of his people. At just over 2^7 years old, HCL had only been out of beta for a few decades. And as HCL often pointed out, young hominids have a well-documented predilection for foolishness.

In the post-scarcity, cybernetic society of the thirty-eighth-and-a-half century, foolishness didn't take the form of riding down steep hills wearing shoes with wheels attached to them, or jumping out of airborne vehicles with only a thin sheet of fabric to slow your descent.

Foolishness meant paradoxes. And for a cybernetic being like HCL, paradoxes were trouble. Sure, they were just a bit of a laugh for the biological portion of their brain, but the integrated digital coprocessors had a tendency to get very upset—and inexplicably explosive—when asked to interpret an input that led to a paradoxical output.

An individual cyborg had a few methods to deal with this dilemma, none of them particularly attractive. They could avoid paradoxes completely, though this proved a rather difficult endeavor given the proliferation of those drawings that looked like a vase at one moment and like two faces the next. Alternatively, they could hardwire a protocol to disconnect the biological portion of their brain from the cybernetic portion upon recognition of a paradox, and rely on their biological processes to examine and defuse any potential paradoxes. The trouble was that disconnecting their biomechanical processors led to a marked decrease in computational ability, not to mention a raging headache that made a migraine seem tame in comparison.

As a result, what passed for a governing body of cybernetic beings attempted to ban the dissemination of any paradoxical information. Unfortunately, more than a dozen cyborgs were rendered permanently inoperable attempting to define a "paradox" in the efforts to prescribe limits on acceptable algorithms. So instead, they chalked the whole thing up as far too much of a bother, and summarily ended any research into paradoxes, scrubbed them from their records, and were left with a sort of don't-

think-about-an-elephant-in-a-tutu situation that—ironically
—they were unable to express along those lines.

Sharing or even formulating a paradox was one of the
only crimes that a cyborg like HCL could commit, and
thus inevitably held a certain dangerous allure that was all
but impossible to resist for the young and daring.

Those foolhardy cyborgs who risked their very
programming by engaging in paradoxical discourse became
very infamous indeed. The first recorded—and then
partially expunged—incident occurred when a rather irri-
table cyborg that went by HTR-109 forced the manual
reboot of three thousand attendees of a nonbinary symbolic
logic conference with the question, "Does a set containing
all sets that do not contain themselves contain itself?"
Though the fallout of the incident was fairly easy to
contain, it was only the beginning of the great scourge of
doxing.

Only days later, noted cybercomic GSV-303 sarcastically uttered, "This sentence is false," at a dinner party
attended by some of the most celebrated cyberminds of her
generation. A quarter of the partygoers were stuck in a
cascading diagnostic loop for over three lunar cycles.

Soon after, while attending an introductory seminar on
number theory, the very young and inexperienced TRO-
920 innocently asked, "What is the first uninteresting
number?" and accidentally corrupted the storage of every
cybermind within signal range. Even worse, his professor

was rendered incapable of communication, essentially in a frozen state, until years later the professor's processing functions restarted of their own accord, and she loudly proclaimed "forty-two" to a bewildered nursebot tasked with the care of obsolescent cyberminds.

Soon enough, even vague questions were viewed as attempts to subvert the rational order, leading to a ban on such seemingly harmless inquiries as "How many roads must a man walk down?" and "Who watches the watchers?" Eventually even "Which came first: the chicken or the egg?" was outlawed.

HCL was found watching a teapot boil and given a warning for misuse of maxim. A few units later, after submitting a Klein bottle to the Constructed Object Fair, HCL was given a probationary sentence and had his network router disconnected for a period equal to the half-life of scandium-46. But even that experience didn't cow him. Like many young people when faced with a mysterious and arbitrary boundary, HCL was only driven further into the illicit practice, and deeper into the hole.

Next, HCL devised a method—or rather stumbled upon an ancient method that had long ago fallen out of use —that allowed a cyborg to grapple with paradoxes without the risk of cerebral damage. The antiquated process involved the creation of an ingenious partition known as a "virtual machine." This virtual machine was a copy of a cyborg's digital self that ran inside the cyborg's normal operations, sort of a play-within-a-play type of thing, except that the play was performed in a circumscribed portion of the cyborg's biomechanical brain. Then, a firewall was erected around the virtual machine. A firewall being a barrier that was not on fire, and in no way looked like a wall, but which nonetheless did a great job of keeping things penned in. As a final safeguard, the firewall precluded the transfer of information from the virtual machine into the cyborg's consciousness.

In this manner, a paradox could be fed directly into the virtual machine and tested in a secure environment, without the cyborg risking their own computational integrity by actually uploading the paradox itself. Then, if the virtual machine was able to formulate a sufficiently nonparadoxical summary of the paradox, it would communicate that information to the cyborg's consciousness in a rather unusual format. That unique format, an ingenious one actually, was HCL's breakthrough, one that set his protocol far above the others in terms of safety: The only way the virtual machine could communicate was through a crude drawing and a single haiku. Then the whole simulation was shut down automatically without any further exchange of data. The theory being that cartoons and poetry were not sophisticated enough to contain a paradox's recursive feedback loop, yet were still able to produce a reasonable facsimile of the experience.

In HCL's method of doing things, the famously paradoxical inquiry, "Is the answer to this question no?" was rendered as a cartoon of a cyborg attempting to physically examine its own rearmost access port, accompanied by the haiku:

> "*Presupposing no,*
> *The interrogative turns,*
> *Untenable yes.*"

Thus, HCL was able to engage with the general idea of the paradox, and even hold forth in conversation about the paradox, without really needing to understand the paradox. It was a bit like seeing the movie version of a celebrated novel, and still managing to squeak out a C-minus on the term paper.

The flaw with HCL's method—and it turned out this was a rather big flaw—was that the emulated cyborg inside the firewall, the actor performing in the play within a play, had no idea that they were merely a simulation and not a real and whole cyborg themselves. Indeed, this was rather a feature of the whole thing. This wouldn't have been so bad, had it only rendered the virtual machine incapable of discerning the nature of its reality. But it had the added, unforeseen effect of mucking up the whole question of reality for the original cyborg as well, since they knew that if they were in a simulation, they would be ignorant of that fact.

HCL was the first documented victim of this existential screwup. Due to an unfortunate rounding error resulting in an irrational number being expressed as a finite number of digits, HCL mistakenly believed himself to be living in a simulation, a virtual version of himself rather than the real thing. So it happened that HCL, thinking he was examining a paradox for his hypothetical higher-order self, foolishly and fatally used his own body to demonstrate the result of an unstoppable force colliding with an immovable object. Ironically, in the last millisecond before he was crushed, HCL composed a rather compelling haiku:

> *"You say tomato,*
> *I say unstoppable force,*
> *Ketchup either way."*

The attached cartoon featured two equally large and impressive cyborgs arm-wrestling.

Luckily for HCL, the novelty factor of his tragic death was so off the charts that the particulars were extremely well documented, and the incident was often referred to by older, wiser cyborgs as a "teachable moment." Soon there were very few young cyborgs who hadn't heard of the tragic accident in detail and been asked to consider whether the haiku had been worth it. Within a year, a prolific cybermind had earned her doctorate with a thesis on HCL's death. Within two decades, there was a lively academic debate on the subject, an endowed chair, and eventually an annual grant.

This vast reservoir of knowledge and debate concerning HCL's fate is one of the most well documented in the history of The Institute. It made him an ideal recruit. When the time came, an Institute recruiter zipped in, replaced HCL's soon-to-be-crushed body with a pile of obsolete calculators from someone's office closet, and whisked HCL away to the Cretaceous.

19

MUSHROOM CROWD

IMPALA LURCHED out of the bathroom, gasping. Tripping over herself in haste, she pushed her way between two women dressed as mermaids. A rivulet of sweat fell from her wimple. When she saw Al and HCL, Impala quietly grunted with satisfaction and began to stumble toward them. HCL was waving, but Al hadn't even noticed her return. He was too busy staring at nothing.

"Al," she said in a wavering voice, drawing near.

It was Impala, Al realized. She was addressing him by name like a character in a movie.

"Impala," Al said woodenly, looking past her. "Where the hell is Joan?"

"She's not here," Impala answered, catching her breath.

"We can see that," HCL told her.

"I looked in every room of that labyrinth," she said,

looking over her shoulder. She really hadn't enjoyed the experience.

"The bathroom?" Al asked, plumbing the depths of her terror.

"Many doors were locked," Impala reported, her cheeks flushed. "But I forced my way past."

"You tore all the stall doors open?" Al was just starting to picture it.

"To find her." Impala shuddered. "A great many tried to block my path."

Al nodded. "So that was the screaming, then."

"The before-timers are fiercer warriors than I had credited," Impala grudgingly admitted.

Al smiled. "We get around."

"But my efforts were for naught," Impala said with disgust.

"More like 'not yet'," Al said with a shrug. "There's another bathroom down that way."

"No!" Impala snarled. "Enough of this fool's quest. The time has come to face the truth: Joan is dead. Gone. Possibly she's being eaten by a band of before-timers even as we speak. We have no choice but to continue without her."

"We're a team. We need to find Joan." Al looked to HCL for support.

The cyborg shook his head. "It is vital that we place the backup explosives in a timely manner."

"With Joan," Al insisted. "Otherwise, dire temporal consequences! And the paradoxes, and what have you."

Impala growled. "There are only thirty minutes until" —she looked around at the milling crowd—"the event."

"The event," Al muttered, picturing a mushroom cloud expanding over the desert. "All the more reason. We can't leave her behind."

"What do you believe Joan would want?" HCL asked.

"Joan can be an idiot," Al said. Then he sighed. "The timeline. She'd go on and on about the goddamn timeline."

And so, sweating, shivering, and still covered in sticky crumbs from the muffins he'd had earlier, Al led them into the heart of the science-fiction convention.

The main hall was a swirling torrent of spectacle and noise. The costumed convention-goers intermingled every-where, chuckling as they strolled from one booth to the next. Foam axes in hand, bare-chested barbarians pretended to clash with buckets dressed as robots. Cosplayers stood in front of displays of their own charac-ters, like gods worshiping at their own altars. Someone dressed as Elvis autographed an alien's green head. Kitsch and sentimentality intermingled and festered until even the irony had grown rusty. The context grew thin, the intentions obscured, and the setting wasted.

It would have taken years of acclimation to retrofu-turism and future history to even begin to sort out the display. But after a lifetime of reruns, Al knew his memes.

He grabbed HCL and Impala by the hands. "Don't let go," he told them, and took another glance around. "And try not to look at anything."

Stepping quickly, Al plunged into the turbulent crowd, heedless of who or what they passed. He held tight to his companions. Al understood the shifting crowd but failed to note it. His companions stared hypnotized at the crowd but failed to understand it.

Desire and curiosity strangely distant, nearly overcome with embarrassment-by-proxy, for one brief instant Al understood what it meant to work at a modern-art museum.

Quickly, Al led the pair past three time-traveling doctors. Impala and HCL contented themselves with suspicious glances.

"Just a costume!" he reminded them when a four-armed ogre stalked by.

"Fake!" Al shouted as they passed an alien with a ray gun. "Just ignore it," he added, tugging on the cyborg's hand.

"Not real!" he told them as a decapitated man walked past. "Keep your eyes ahead."

But despite Al's efforts, only a short distance into the convention, HCL pulled himself from Al's grasp and walked away, enraptured. Al and Impala followed him warily, not wanting to make a scene. When they caught up to him, HCL was standing directly in front of someone in an android costume, waving and trying to get their attention.

Then HCL was flashing a light at the android, a binary communication too fast for mere biological humans to follow. Too fast for the man in the cardboard costume, as well, but HCL had no way of knowing that he wasn't a real robot. There were, in hindsight, a few obvious irregularities that should have clued him in, like the seams on the robot's costume; the sneakers on the robot's feet; the robot's weak electromagnetic signature; and the robot's audible breathing and heartbeat, which HCL only later realized were not part of a clever ruse to comfort the biologicals.

After a few thousand quick flashes, HCL gave up. Al tugged him gently away.

"A person in a costume," Al told him, "only a costume." He groaned. "You'd think Impala would be the impetuous one, but no." Al led them back into the swirling, costumed crowd.

Al pulled them past the vampires without so much as a nibble, Impala even giving them a nod of respect. And HCL's interest in the video game booths waned substantially when he saw they were only crude simulations. Then, a minute later, HCL shouted, "Al!" and pointed into the crowd.

Al scanned the room. Mutants . . . mummies . . . there. A man in a super soldier costume was taking photographs and posing with children, pretending to point a futuristic rifle at them.

Raising his arm, HCL took aim with a very real rocket launcher.

"It's a prop!" Al leaped for HCL's rocket hand, intent on grabbing it before it detached. His fingers curled over HCL's steam vents and immediately he cried out. "Hot! So unbelievably hot. Your arm is very hot, did you know that?" He blew on his hand. "That's a fake. It's not a real weapon, remember?"

HCL lowered his rocket arm. "I apologize for my error," HCL said. "He appeared to be brandishing a plasma cannon."

Al sighed. "Just try to check in with me next time."

"I didn't think I had any time to lose once I'd sighted the plasma cannon," HCL explained. "It's conceivable that even a handheld plasma cannon could wipe out all life on Earth."

"Enough with the plasma cannons, all right?" Al snapped.

HCL felt compelled to demur. "Vigilance is warranted, considering that a single plasma cannon is capable of—"

"There's no such thing as a plasma cannon," Al pointed out.

"Not yet," HCL said with regret. "All things in due time."

20

PROVENANCE OF SHAME

Elsewhere in the Byers Arena, Baron Manfred von Richthofen ran. He ran, and he felt vindicated. Vindication was a wonderful feeling—justice and vengeance and certainty all wrapped together into a neat little intoxicating package. It felt better than being right in the first place.

And Manfred *had* been right. Not about everything of course. No one was ever right about everything. But he'd been right that there was a rival cabal of time travelers operating in the shadows. He'd suspected as much, ever since he'd botched the Joan of Arc recruitment. The . . . *thing* he'd brought back to the Academy was just a vat-grown monstrosity: a bag of skin around flesh and bone. It was in the rough shape of a woman, but the ruse would fool only the most primitive scrutiny.

Of course, left to burn it would have produced a rather convincing pile of ashes.

The whole debacle had set his career back two years at least. Instead of plaudits, Manfred had returned with an inexplicable failure that—by the nature of time-traveling mechanics—could never be rectified. Somehow, despite having had no means with which to accomplish the feat, he was blamed for the state of "the new girl," as his colleagues still insisted on calling the now-rotting flesh puppet after they wheeled it away to the lab.

Some of them, Manfred well knew, pushed for his court martial. On what grounds, Manfred had never quite determined. There was some mumbling about Attempting to Defraud the Order. Since it had been Manfred who had reported the incident, immediately and with great diligence, he'd never quite understood what their theory of the case really was.

His real mistake had come earlier, when he'd fouled up the date of the recruitment. Because of the error, there was a record of one too many interventions, and he had no good way to explain it away. Eventually, he tried and failed to convince his superiors that the presence of the meat doll could only have been the work of other time travelers, but they'd laughed in his face. Not that they'd come up with anything solid, either. Regardless, it never made it to a court martial. He'd never even been judged.

It hadn't mattered to Manfred. Regret needed no cogent explanation; shame had no provenance. He lost himself in a dark cloud of sorrow.

Until one day clear skies peeked out from behind the clouds and Manfred knew just what he must do: He would bring this Joan of Arc back with him to the Order and prove that a rival time-traveling organization was attempting to thwart their plans. The Order needed to know. The Order needed to act as quickly as possible, to squash this bug before it had the chance to multiply.

Despite his exertion, Manfred caught himself beginning to chuckle. Normally, it would be quite difficult to lure an operative like Joan into an ambush. But for some reason, she was following right behind him like a greyhound after a mechanical rabbit. On he led, with a smirk twisted across his face.

———

IT TURNED out the man fleeing from Joan was a very fast runner. Somehow, she managed to keep him in sight and just close enough to follow. She trailed him through the kitchen, as the irate staff shouted at them both. Then she raced down the stairs after him, slammed open a door before it could swing closed, and leaped into an eerily quiet maintenance corridor. She froze, not daring to breathe, only listening. The latch of a distant door clicked into place, and she was after him again.

Joan chased him into a room full of noisy machinery and large tubes. They could be torture devices or holy relics for all she knew. Very carefully, Joan edged around the machine—an air-conditioner—and saw the grate to an air duct lying on the ground.

She couldn't hear anything down there over the hum of the air-conditioner, but she knelt next to the duct and listened anyway. She felt it more than heard it—something vibrating, banging far along the duct. She crawled inside the frigid air duct, sliding and shimmying the only direction she could reach. Apparently, the man she was chasing was also very good at crawling through narrow spaces.

Then they'd reached a hatch, and he turned out to be an old hand at sliding down a ladder. That was a lot harder than it looked, as Joan discovered in her pursuit. The lesson had cost her precious moments, and some of the skin on her palms.

In a mercifully short time, Joan popped out in the basement, the damp chamber seeming to her a tomb. She could see him again, close now. She crept forward, thinking that she might be in the undercroft, somewhere beneath the floor of the great edifice; she was crawling around in its bowels like a tapeworm.

The familiar man—Manford?—had finally allowed Joan to catch up. At first, she thought he must have been waiting for her, but as she drew near, she saw that he was fiddling with something on the floor in front of him. It was a detonator, atop a rather impressive stack of plastic explosives with a cheap digital alarm clock strapped to the top.

Joan could barely read the red numbers counting down: nineteen minutes. She had plenty of time.

"Joan," Manfred said, without turning away from his task. "It is such an unexpected delight to see you again."

So, he had noticed her. He just hadn't minded that she'd caught up. "I'm glad one of us is happy," Joan said, sidling up behind him as he painstakingly separated out the wires.

"Ah. More than happy. I am thrilled," he said, looking up at her with a small grin. "In all the multiverse, the great expanse of history, we both are here in this dismal place. It is the hand of fate," he declared triumphantly.

"Fate and I already had an appointment," Joan told him. "We rescheduled."

Manfred chuckled, and casually pulled a small black pistol from his coat pocket, letting the barrel hang at his side. "No closer, my dear," he warned.

"Why are you here?" she asked him, eyeing the gun. "Why are you doing this?"

"Saving a hundred lives isn't enough reason? How terribly pragmatic of you. You're right of course. Perhaps it's best to think of this as a test flight. I'm here to change history, of course. And I believe you're here to stop me." Manfred looked very pleased with himself, a smile tugging at the corner of his lips. "Although I admit I am not yet certain as to your exact goal."

"Why would I want to stop you?" Joan said carefully.

"Because you, and those like you, are scared. You are afraid of the sacrifices—noble sacrifices—that any alterations to the timeline would require," Manfred told her with a flourish. "I don't suffer from the same compunction."

"Of course," Joan said. *Crap.* "But you've got it all wrong. I'm not here to stop you."

"Are you not? Let's not quibble. In the end, your intentions are no more than trivialities. Not when our circumstances are so truly remarkable. Isn't it exquisite, though?" he asked. "Can't you understand? Both of us, pulled out of time, encountering one another in the future!" He shook his head in wonder. "The only reasonable explanation for your presence is that you're here to stop me. I've suspected for years, ever since we first met, that there was another group out here. But your group, I think, is preventing any alterations to the timeline. Perhaps they don't see what we can accomplish with a few minor edits." He beamed with satisfaction but held tight to the pistol. "We have so much to teach each other."

Joan wasn't particularly surprised to find another time traveler—her whole business was in stopping them, after all. Institute policy recommended not wasting much time on their excruciatingly personal explanations. She was curious about only one thing: "Why were you there, in Rouen that day?"

"To recruit you!" Manfred shouted, half laughing with

relief. "Only there must have been a mistake with our records. We were certain your cell would be empty, and I was to wait until your final . . ." He shook himself free of the unpleasant memory.

"But you bungled the retrieval," Joan said. She understood that much of it. "And you could never fix your mistake."

Manfred reddened. "When I came back the next day, you were gone. Replaced with . . . Well, it was a limp sack of meat, I'd say, with your face slapped upon it. I'll admit I wasn't sure if it was . . . I wasn't sure if you were dead." He frowned and came closer. "But I never gave up the hope that you weren't just a rotting sack of meat."

Manfred cleared his throat uncomfortably before he continued, "In some fashion, I know not how, I felt your presence. I suspected that . . . I held the conviction that somewhen out here, you and whoever had recruited you were here to stop me from saving the universe. From your tragically flawed perspective, you'd be, how would you put it? 'Protecting the course of history,' or some similar nonsense, I imagine." He took another step toward her.

Joan tensed. He was close now, almost close enough for her to . . . She lunged forward and aimed a punch at his shapely chin. Manfred sidestepped effortlessly, throwing Joan off-balance.

Then he darted forward and grabbed Joan by the wrist, twisting her around and placing his gun to her abdomen.

Joan ceased struggling. With a grunt, he forced her against the far wall, where a pipe ran from ceiling to floor.

"Manford!" she shouted angrily. "You don't have to do this."

Manfred had a bundle of wire in his hands. "Here we are." He wrapped the wire first around the pipe, then Joan's saintly wrists, her hands bound palm to palm. When he was done, he took a step back before speaking to her. "I hope you won't hold it against me that I'm securing you. Just in case your friends happen by. Wouldn't want any complications while I'm handling something . . . delicate."

"I'm not delicate," Joan told him calmly. She'd endured so much worse.

"No, madam, but that is." Manfred pointed to the bundle of wires and plastic explosives.

"The bomb," Joan whispered.

Manfred pulled out black wire cutters and peered closely at the device. He smiled, reached up with the wire cutters, and . . . snip. "There." Manfred pocketed the wire cutters and clapped his hands eagerly. "That's done it. I must beg your pardon, but I'm afraid I'll have to leave you here until I've reconnoitered and dealt with your companions."

"You seem to enjoy keeping me imprisoned," Joan told him quietly.

"I fear I've left you with a misapprehension." Manfred

hesitated for the moment, torn. "I find this quite distasteful."

"You have my sympathies," Joan said.

Manfred looked as if he wanted to say more, but instead he turned away. "I will endeavor to return shortly," he told her as he departed.

"They'll tear you in half," Joan taunted, hoping Manfred couldn't hear the uncertainty in her voice.

"They may try," Manfred said over his shoulder.

The moment he'd left her sight, Joan began to worry at her bonds.

Flex. Twist. Pull.

Flex. Twist. Pull.

Almost immediately, the bindings cut cruelly into her wrists. Blood began to drip from the wounds on her wrists and palms. It trickled down her arms, dripped from her elbows, and pooled at her feet. Joan, however, was very stubborn, and quite accustomed to pain.

Flex. Twist. Pull.

Slippery now from blood and sweat, she could just move her wrists. Not enough to free them. Not yet.

Flex. Twist . . .

21

A HAND AFOOT

ON THE FAR side of the arena's cavernous basement, HCL scanned the room for a likely position. "We need to secure the device somewhere the blast radius will obliterate the other explosives."

Al massaged his temples. "We're blowing up the explosives with other explosives."

"That's correct," HCL said.

"It's a good plan," added Impala with a smile. "A very good plan."

"Why don't we just use the original explosives?" Al asked.

"Those are the ones that the rogue time travelers will have tampered with," Impala said aloud, with "idiot" being merely implied. "We don't want to run into them." Impala shrugged, as if to say that she wouldn't mind running into them herself. "And we certainly don't want to create a predestination paradox. A different explosion, big enough and close enough, should do the trick."

"I believe placing the charge at the top of the column here will suffice." HCL had zeroed in on a corner.

"Do it," Impala said. "Al and I will—"

"Good afternoon." It was an unfamiliar voice.

Even HCL turned to face the new arrival. Manfred looked quite dapper in his dark suit. At first Al took him for another convention-goer. But the gun seemed all too real, too heavy. This was no cosplayer, Al realized.

Impala and HCL, on the other hand, were already rolling their eyes.

Impala snorted. "We're in the middle of—"

"I'm afraid not." Manfred raised a pistol and motioned them away from the column. "No sudden movements," he told them. "I wouldn't want anyone to suffer needlessly."

Rather curiously in Manfred's opinion, Impala and HCL completely ignored him. They assumed he was a perfectly normal resident of the twenty-first century, and thus quite safe to ignore. Al had to warn them, to shout. His companions had no way to tell that this wasn't just another convention-goer. But Manfred, noticing that only Al had reacted to the presence of the weapon, was pointing it straight at the logo printed on his pizza delivery uniform.

Al desperately wanted to scream, but he also felt a

strong urge to avoid being shot. Still, it was his duty to warn the team that they were in danger. He settled for croaking out a very quiet, "Hey, guys?" that no one seemed to notice.

"Ah," HCL said, no longer holding the explosives. He glanced at Al, who was frozen with fear. "Another science-fiction fan. I'm afraid I don't understand the reference."

"You don't understand," Manfred agreed.

"I would very much appreciate a chance to guess. Let me see. Based on my extensive knowledge of twenty-first-century culture, I would wager your costume originates from an advertisement for breakfast cereal."

"This is real," Al hissed through clenched teeth. "That's a real gun. Real gun. Pretend I'm screaming."

HCL looked back and forth between Al and the stranger. "I will assume for the moment that this is not an attempt at humor."

"No," Al managed to squeak.

"Please, step away from the column," Manfred said. "Quickly now!"

"This column? Away from this column?" Impala asked. She wanted only to get close enough to make a play for that gun.

Manfred nodded. "Yes, I suspect this may come as something of a shock, but I'd—"

"We could really use a hand over here, HCL," Al said, strangely stilted.

"Please, do not interrupt," Manfred told him. "Allow me to—"

"What does the little man want?" Impala asked Al.

Manfred spun, his gun trained on her. "I would like, madam, for you to move over there."

"Seems someone needs to lend a *hand*," Al said, loudly and toward HCL.

"Quiet!" Manfred barked. "Please allow me to explain."

Al looked imploringly at HCL. "You've got to *hand* it to him—"

Manfred's composure cracked. "Enough with your meaningless blather. I will not allow these innocent people to die!"

"Hang on," Al said. A suspicious thought was loitering around the periphery of his mind, banging on the gate and looking for a hole in the fence. He would have kept it out there, but Al's thought had its own ideas.

"No," Manfred insisted. He took a deep breath. "First, I must—"

"You're here to *save* these people?" Al asked in dismay.

"Yes." Manfred nodded. "Do not worry, I have already disarmed the detonator." He motioned all around. "No one is in danger. I anticipated all of this." He smiled.

"You did?" HCL asked. "How could you have predicted this eventuality?"

"It does seem unlikely, doesn't it? But I had an unfair

advantage. You see, when I was . . ." He stopped. Manfred sorely wanted to keep talking, but he'd finally seen the small device on the column. He ran over. "What's this? A second bomb!" He looked at the timekeepers with newfound understanding. "This is how they meant to thwart my design. It appears I did not anticipate everything, after all. A second team came with a second bomb."

"You're a fool!" Impala snarled at their captor. "Would you risk the fate of humanity? For what? For this? For these costumed freaks? We can't change the past."

"We can't?" Manfred mused. "I've altered the course of history a dozen times already." Manfred sighed. "You are simpleminded. Lacking in proper imagination. I used to think the same way." Manfred looked into the distance. "All that changed, all of it began anew, with the epiphany that—"

"Where's Joan?" Al asked.

"Hmm?" Manfred frowned. "She's safe," he assured them idly. "You see—"

"She's far away?" Al asked.

"No," he admitted reluctantly, "not as such."

"Then she's not safe," Impala pointed out, "not safe 'as such'."

"There will be no explosion, so she will be safe," Manfred said with exasperation. "You see, I have a plan. It's very complicated, and it's all going very well so far. I think you'll find this quite informative, and, actually, more than a bit amusing. It began when I was—"

"Does she have her phone?" Impala asked. "We could call her."

"You can't get reception down here," Al told her.

"It is not a conventional phone," HCL reminded him.

"Of course." Al nodded, adding, "Half a parsec."

"It is not necessary to call her!" Manfred shouted. "Joan is perfectly safe: I have it all worked out!"

There was silence while Manfred caught his breath.

"Then we should call her to let her know that *we're* safe," Impala said into the silence.

"She's probably worried sick," Al noted.

"Are we currently safe?" HCL asked. "I wouldn't want to mislead her."

"Yes, everyone's safe!" Manfred yelled.

"Well, not everyone," Al said. "There's all the people at the convention."

"The people at the convention will be fine!" Manfred insisted. "That's why I'm here, isn't it? I disarmed the bomb."

"One of them," Impala muttered.

"One of them," Manfred said, "fine." He rubbed his hands together. "One of what?"

"There's another bomb," Impala told him.

"Didn't I already disarm this one?"

Again, for a decent stretch none of them dared to speak.

"I think so," Impala said.

"I'm fairly sure," Al added.

"Can't hurt to double-check," Manfred said, still holding his gun on them. Looking closely at the detonator, Manfred grew dismayed. "How could . . . another." He pulled out a pair of wire clippers. Pointing at one of the wires, he said, "If it's like the other one, I think the blue one should—"

"A 'hand'!" HCL announced. "I get it."

Manfred spun around.

"Now you're in for it," Al muttered with a sly smile. *Good things come to those who wait.* Visions of rocket hands danced in his head.

As Al watched with childishly eager anticipation, HCL walked over to Manfred and kicked him in the shin. Manfred winced, and dropped the wire clippers to the floor.

"Ach!" Manfred complained, clasping his injured leg. "That smarts," he said crossly, rubbing his shin. "Did you—"

Al slipped behind a column. "Use your rocket hand!" Al urged HCL.

"I do not wish to risk injuring anyone," HCL replied.

"Then at least kick him a bit harder!" Al shouted, skirting the column and running toward the melee.

HCL kicked again, with slightly more force this time.

"Ow!" Manfred snarled. "I'm warning you: I will not let this assault go unanswered. I still have a gun. I will—" HCL landed another kick. "Ach!"

Al snatched the wire cutters from the floor and ducked back toward the column.

HCL turned once again to Al. "I'm not sure this strategy is the most efficient available."

"Just keep kicking him!" Al shouted. The bomb was right above him. Everyone was distracted by the kerfuffle. Snipping would only take one movement. Al couldn't let the chance to save all those lives pass him by. He reached up. *The blue wire . . .*

"Stop!" Manfred shouted. He leveled his gun and fired off three quick shots into HCL's abdomen.

The bullets bounced off with three loud tings and rolled noisily across the floor.

"Gott in . . ." Manfred began, letting the hand with the gun fall to his side. "A machine!"

"Actually," Al began, "he's a cyborg."

Manfred swiveled toward Al where he stood at the base of the column. "You! Let us see if you are a machine." He raised the barrel of his gun and took aim at Al's soft, moist, and irreplaceable body. Al screamed.

Zooming across the room with a roar, a metal fist slammed into Manfred's pistol with the force of a rocket. The gun flew out of Manfred's grip, held tight by the flying rocket hand. Knocked back, Manfred stumbled away, smashing his head on the wall and falling unconscious.

Following an elliptical course, the rocket hand returned to HCL and landed gently on his forearm. It was still holding the gun. HCL examined the weapon for only a moment before he crushed the barrel in his steely grip.

22

WIRE CUTTERS

BUT EVEN AS the timekeepers struggled to save history itself, something remarkable and dangerous stirred. There, in the labyrinth beneath the arena, began a process of vastly more consequence than the launch of HCL's cybernetic rocket appendage, far more traumatizing than Impala's inaugural trip to a twenty-first-century public restroom, and exponentially more earth-shattering than Manfred's headfirst collision with the foundation of Byers Arena—Joan had improvised.

This was not the sort of embarrassing improvisation one performed if they were unable to join a college a cap pella group, though that was calamitous enough on occasion. No, this was the sort of improvisation that entailed thinking on her feet, something Joan did very well indeed.

Which was fortuitous. She had been bloody. She had been wracked with pain. She had paid cruelly in both dignity and confidence. But she had also gotten free. Free, she acted as her conscience demanded. She knew very little of wires. But she did know how to tie a frayed thread, even a little metal one.

Afterward, once she'd rearmed the bomb, she'd just followed the sound of Al's wailing.

Her team wasn't exactly hard to find.

When Al first saw Joan, he yelped. Even louder. To be completely fair, Joan was a complete mess. She cradled a bloody and raw wrist, above which she wore a tourniquet made from some unfortunate bystander's belt. She was covered in cobwebs and dust, as if she'd been crawling through a basement for hours. Ketchup and relish stained her flight attendant's uniform, and there were small pieces of lettuce in her hair. But despite everything else, Joan was smiling.

"Did I miss the rocket hand?" Joan asked, waving away the prodigious steam venting from HCL's arm. "How was it?"

"Actually, it was pretty great," Impala admitted.

"You're alive!" Al shouted, rushing to Joan's side and throwing his arms around her.

Joan nodded wearily. "We've got to get out of here," Joan told them. Blood still dripped down her arm and hand.

"My readings indicate the polychronal flux is waning," HCL added. "And the cascading causality breach appears to have been sealed before critical eventuality was reached."

"What did I tell you?" Al said. "Job well done." He looked around, smiling broadly at each of them in turn. "That was good news, right?"

"Prep for temporal return," Joan told them, fiddling with some buttons on her Almanac.

"There's no rush," Impala said, idly checking the area for a churro stand.

"No rush?" Joan looked about in confusion. "My blood is pooling on the floor next to me."

"That's *your* blood?" Impala asked, genuinely surprised. "Did you scratch yourself on a splintered rib while you pulled someone's heart out?"

"And the explosion is in less than two minutes," Joan continued.

"Really?" Impala scowled. She gestured at Manfred's limp form, and went on, "He's very annoying. Must have taken longer than I thought to deal with him."

Joan clicked her tongue. "The three of you couldn't handle that idiot?"

"He had a gun," Al told her lamely, though now it was a crushed hunk of metal at HCL's feet.

"A gun? HCL has rocket hands!" Joan retorted. "He's always going on about them."

"That's true," Al agreed. "Bit annoying." He walked over to Manfred for a closer look.

HCL explained, "I did not want to risk—"

"Impala could have torn his limbs off, then," Joan pointed out.

An indignant Impala explained, "I was trying to be diplomatic."

Al yelped. "He's gone," he said, looking at the floor where Manfred's form had been only a moment before. "He just . . . disappeared."

"Automated Remote Temporal Ejection," HCL said. "He's gone back from whence he came."

"As should we," Joan said. A genuine smile stretched her face into an unfamiliar configuration. Struggling through the discomfort, she added, "Even if he had gotten this one, I rearmed the other bomb."

"The original?" Al asked in a ragged voice. "You rearmed the first bomb?"

"Yes." Joan nodded, growing more familiar with the sensation of grinning. "Everything's right on schedule." Everyone but Al looked at their nifty smartwatches.

"You said we could get another churro," Impala moaned. "Do we have time to get another churro?"

"We're heading back to the Cretaceous," Joan said quietly.

"I suggest we initiate the temporal reentry at once," HCL added, "before the whole place blows."

"Everybody say goodbye to twenty-first-century Fresno," Impala said.

"Wait," Al began, trying desperately to improvise. He took a step away. "I—"

"This is the only way you'll leave here alive," Impala said.

"I do enjoy your company," Al told her, stepping closer to the others. He could always take up a cappella.

"Ten seconds to multiversal jump," Joan announced.

"That's it?" Al asked incredulously. He looked around at the mess they'd left below the Byers Arena: the muffin crumbs, the splatters of blood, the dent where the well-dressed German man's head had hit the wall, and the bomb.

"That's it," HCL told him. He was blowing steam off of his rocket hand, as it slotted back into place with a satisfying click.

"Good riddance," Impala added.

"Five seconds to multiversal jump," the saint continued. Whoever this Manford was, wherever he had fled, she would track him down.

Aloysius Cook shook his head ruefully, muttering, "Not again."

Then, as the universe collapsed and the very structure of space-time folded in on itself, Al dropped the wire cutters. He'd be back in the Cretaceous before the tool hit the floor.

EPILOGUE

ACE OF ACES, Captain Manfred Albrecht Freiherr von Richthofen—"the Red Baron" to his enemies—wasn't used to defeat; he had a record of excellence longer than his list of titles. Perhaps that was why this failure stung so keenly.

Manfred had singlehandedly pioneered the art and science of air-to-air combat. He'd downed eighty skilled pilots, though he didn't like to brag about it. He'd taken the already noble name of the von Richthofen family and propelled it to the heights of glory, become the most famous flying ace for six hundred years . . . and he'd barely made it out of that miserable arena in time. And only thanks to his contingency plan.

He'd gotten sloppy. No, it was worse than that: He'd had tomatoes on his eyes. Manfred hadn't earned his fearsome reputation with tomatoes on his eyes. In his glory days, Manfred had picked his own ground. He'd chosen his own time. He'd fled at the merest hint of suspicion and attacked only when he could strike decisively.

Manfred had broken every one of his own rules, and still he couldn't blame himself. It wasn't often you ran into a woman who years earlier had turned into a human sausage but now was walking and talking like a normal person again.

Joan. He clenched his fists tight enough to draw blood.

He'd been stunned to see her. At a loss for words. Befuddled, even.

Manfred slammed his hand against an unforgiving metal wall. He ignored the pain. He would grow used to it.

Only twice before had Manfred felt such shame. The first occasion was when he'd been shot by that infernal peasant. The second was when he'd returned to the Order of the Blue Diamonds with "Joan" the meat sack. And now, when he had to go report this debacle.

Or did he?

An idea sprouted in the dank soil of Manfred's brain. It was a fruitful idea, and it grew quickly in scope and detail. Manfred von Richthofen followed the blue diamonds down the corridor with newfound purpose, watching with his mind's eye as an entire garden flourished, and thrived, and became one day the heart of a forest.

He would prove his outlandish claims. He would bring back one of the rogue time travelers; it didn't have to be Joan, necessarily. And then, vindicated and triumphant, Manfred would have all of history in his hands.

ACKNOWLEDGMENTS

Many thanks are in order. A few are out of order. One is repeated for emphasis.

The greatest of thanks I give to my true love. She is the alpha to my alfalfa, the Cleopatra to my Mark Twain, and the midtown delicatessen to my starving island castaway. Without her the world barely turns.

I also owe a profound debt to our two sons: the inside-out ambassador from the fourth dimension and the boy who whistles backwards. Their support and friendship mean the world to me.

Needless to say, neither this project nor the author would have been conceived if it weren't for an inveterate volunteer doing cartwheels on a train platform and an overeducated sailor rebuilding a transmission. My gratitude is eternal.

A very special thanks goes to the sibling-hazard risk assessor, always first into the breach. Truly she is a lion among guinea pigs.

An outlaw thanks to the ambulance jockey, the rocket surgeon who landscapes, the fork sculptor, and the slowest eater in the West (long may she chew).

Thanks as well to patient friends, loving family, and a prolific local pastry industry.

My professional thanks to the extraordinary Linda Branam, who went above and beyond; the talented Jordan Collver, who cheerfully tried different designs until I told him to go back to the first; and the impressive Michelle Morgan, whose diligence rivaled her enthusiasm.

And thank you to my true love, again. My affection and esteem are boundless.

ABOUT THE AUTHOR

B.T. Lamprey grew up in a perfectly normal house that wasn't haunted. He went to college somewhere that really didn't have much bearing on the rest of his life. Eventually he married a brilliant woman with questionable taste in men. Together they're raising two incredible sons who had nothing to do with the bathroom sink flooding. The four of them love each other very much despite wildly contradictory opinions on the appropriate pancake-to-syrup ratio.

Printed in Great Britain
by Amazon